AF485528

THE FEAR OF DROWNING

Book Three in **THE FEAR OF** Series

S.C. Sterling

N/B Books

Copyright © 2026 by Scott C. Sterling
All rights reserved. Published in the United States by N/B Books.

Book Design by Charles Layton

Ways to connect with Scott:
www.scsterling.com
sc@scsterling.com

ISBN: 979-8-9897265-3-0

THE FEAR
OF DROWNING

ZERO

Anna knocked lightly on the door, the sound barely loud enough for her to hear, let alone anyone else. As she stood motionless, her heart thumped against her chest.

She'd heard the rumors, but had been in denial she'd ever be called upon, just like someone receiving a cancer diagnosis.

As she was about to step away, a voice said, "Please come in."

When Anna opened the door, she found Kenneth sitting on the edge of the bed, notepad in his lap, moving his finger across the page as he read. After a long pause, he closed the notepad and placed it at his feet.

In the room was the bed, a Bible next to a pistol on the nightstand, and a guitar leaning against the wall. Behind the bed was a small window with the shades closed. A musty scent hung in the air, reminiscent of a week-old pile of damp towels.

"I said come in," Kenneth said, a little louder.

Anna glanced down the hallway, contemplating escape, but she knew she'd never make it past the guards.

As she began taking half steps toward him, he raised his hand. "I prefer my privacy, so please shut the door," he said, gesturing with his fingers.

"Okay," Anna whispered, closing it behind her.

"Now sit," Kenneth said, patting the mattress.

Anna made her way to the bed and sat at arm's length. She'd seen Kenneth countless times, but never this close, and never alone.

"What do you prefer, Anna or Annabelle?"

"It doesn't matter."

"Of course it does. Your name is very important to who you are as a person. Do you honestly not care what people call you?"

"I don't know," she said uneasily.

"I'm sensing some anxiety. Do I scare you?"

"Yeah, a little. I'm sorry for saying that."

Kenneth chuckled. "It's okay. There is nothing to worry about, I promise. I'm as harmless as a caterpillar." He placed his hand on her back, then ran his fingers up and down her spine. "Do you believe me?"

"Yes," the girl said, nodding feverishly.

"Good. I believe trust is fundamental to any relationship. I wouldn't be where I'm at without trust, and if I wasn't here, neither would your family, or your friends, or your classmates, or anyone in town. This community is built on trust, and that all starts with me."

He removed his hand and rested it in his lap. "And if you don't trust me, we can't be friends. Do you want to be friends?"

"I guess," she whispered.

"Good. So, let's try this again. Do you prefer Anna or Annabelle?"

"Anna."

He smiled. "I wasn't going to say anything, but I prefer Anna as well. It is a very pretty name."

Anna nodded.

"And since we're friends now, there is nothing to be scared of, right? Nothing at all."

"Yes, I guess so," she muttered.

"Then why are you so far away?"

"I don't know."

"Please, come closer," Kenneth said, patting the mattress again.

Anna faked a smile, then shuffled over, leaving a few inches between them. He wrapped his arm around her waist and pulled her to him. As the room turned silent, Anna fixated on the door, praying someone would kick it down and rescue her.

Kenneth started humming a melody. After a few bars, he pointed to the guitar. "Do you enjoy when I play?"

"I guess."

He glared down at her.

"I mean, I've only heard you play a couple songs, but what I've heard I've liked."

"Did you know I was in a band when I was younger?"

"No, I didn't."

"I was. It feels like a lifetime ago. Me and some friends covered songs from the Beatles and The Beach Boys." He paused for a moment, seemingly lost in thought. "Do you like those bands?"

Unsure, Anna said, "I've heard the names before, but I don't know any of their songs."

"Yes, that's right. Maybe someday I'll play you some of their records. And speaking of music, your mother told me you want to learn how to play guitar. Is that true?"

"Yes, I've mentioned it to her a few times."

Kenneth leaned his head back and took a deep breath. "Good. Music is what separates us from other species, and something that can unite the worst of enemies. It is vital to our existence."

He picked up the guitar and sat back down. "Would you like me to teach you?"

"That would be nice."

"Great, your first lesson starts right now. I'm going to teach you two chords."

After a deep exhale, Anna took the guitar with timid hands. It was big in her lap, and she repositioned it a few times until she felt comfortable.

"Here, let me see your left hand." He took her index and middle fingers and placed them on the second and third strings of the second fret. "Now take this with your right hand," he said, holding a pick. "Okay, now, strum all the strings."

At first, she barely touched the pick to the strings, like she was afraid she'd break something.

"Perfect, now just play it a little louder. Really come down on them."

She glanced up, and he nodded. She lowered her head and placed the pick on the top string, then after a moment, she brought it down with all her might. The chord echoed throughout the room.

"That's it, that is an E Minor. Your first chord!" he said.

Anna snickered, and for the first time since she'd entered the room, she thought maybe she'd escape unscathed.

"Don't stop now, keep going!" Kenneth said, gesturing with his index finger in a circular motion.

After a minute or so, Kenneth held up his hand, and she stopped playing. "Now I'm going to show you a G Major. So, the last chord was an E Minor, and this is a G Major." He repeated both chords a few times, then repositioned her fingers on the guitar.

As Anna played, Kenneth tapped on his thigh to keep rhythm. Then he called out the first chord. She stopped, then carefully moved her fingers before strumming again. He continued calling out the two chords, and with each change, her confidence and proficiency grew.

"Did you enjoy that?" he said, placing the guitar back against the wall.

"Yes, very much," she said, without hesitation.

"I can see you have a natural talent, and if I'm being honest, I don't think I've ever seen anyone catch on so quickly." He winked at her.

She thanked him repeatedly.

"So, here's an idea. What if I gave you weekly lessons?"

"Really? I would love that more than anything."

"Yes, but you have to promise me that once we start, you won't quit."

"I promise I won't."

"Let's shake on it," Kenneth said, offering his hand.

As they shook, he leered down at her. The sound of their breathing filled the room. Twice, she tried to break off the shake, but he didn't let go.

"Your hands are very soft."

"Umm, thank you," she said.

Kenneth leaned down and kissed her head. "The main reason I requested you is because I wanted to personally wish you a Happy Birthday."

"Thank you."

"How was it?"

Confused, Anna shrugged. "How was what?"

"Your special day?"

"It was fine, I guess."

Kenneth chuckled. "You guess? I feel like you're not being honest with me. Was something wrong?"

"I just wish the cake was strawberry, that's all."

Kenneth nodded and picked up the notepad. After removing a pen from the spine, he flipped to the middle of the book and began writing. Anna averted her eyes, as if seeing what was written on the paper would turn her into stone.

"Next year you'll get strawberry, I promise."

"Thank you," she whispered.

"Well, I have one more surprise for you." Kenneth pulled an unmarked box from under the bed and placed it in her lap. "It is a very special present from me to you."

Anna looked down at it, then up at him.

"Open it," he said.

Carefully, she placed her hands on both ends of the box and slowly pulled the lid up, revealing a yellow prairie dress.

"Well, do you like it?"

"Yes, thank you," she said, her legs trembling. "I didn't think I was allowed to wear anything that isn't white."

"Well, I make the rules, and when you're with me, it's allowed."

Kenneth removed the dress, tossed the box onto the floor, then draped it in front of them.

"It is a very beautiful dress, for a very beautiful girl. In fact, I'd like you to model it for me. Would you do that?"

Anna fixated on the floor, breathing through pursed lips. After about ten seconds, Kenneth asked again, this time loud enough that anyone on the other side of the door could've heard.

"Where can I change?" Anna muttered.

"Right here is fine."

"I don't know if I feel comfortable doing—"

"Remember, we're friends."

Anna started to smile, but it quickly vanished.

"Thirteen is an important age. Very important. You're

not a girl anymore. You're a woman. Do you feel like one?"

Anna started to answer, but each time she had to stop after a few syllables. Finally, she said, "I don't know. I guess."

"Have you ever kissed anyone?" Kenneth said, rubbing her thigh in a slow, circular motion.

"No," she said, starting to blush.

"You don't have to feel embarrassed. Most girls your age haven't kissed a boy. It is perfectly normal. If you can believe it, I myself didn't kiss anyone until I was a little older than you."

Anna swallowed hard, gripped by fear. Her mind raced, remembering all the rumors she'd heard. If half of them were true, she'd rather be dead.

"Would you like me to teach you how to kiss?"

"I don't feel well. Can I please go home?"

As Anna shifted on the bed, there was a loud creak, as if one of the slats beneath the mattress had broken. She flinched, but Kenneth didn't move, almost as though he'd had a premonition the noise was coming.

"Do you know your parents asked me to invite you here? In fact, they begged me. Do you know why they want you here?" he said, his voice rough.

"Because you are the leader."

"That is correct," he said, cracking his knuckles. "And do you know what my job as the leader is?"

"I don't, umm— I don't know if, umm, anyone has told me. I'm sorry."

Kenneth smiled. "It is to keep every person in this community safe from harm, and the only way that happens is if everyone follows my command. Otherwise, outsiders could come in and break apart everything we've built. Everything would vanish into nothing. Everything. And they would not stop until Echo Canyon was in complete ruins. Is that something you want?"

"No," Anna cried, staring up at the ceiling, tears streaming down her cheeks.

"Then you must obey every word I say. And I mean everything. I don't care if it's something as simple as not watching TV, or abstaining from caffeine, or not cheating on a test, or not lying to an elder. All rules must be obeyed."

"Yes, yes! I'll obey everything you say. I'm so sorry, I was just confused."

"Stand! Stand in front of me!"

Anna pushed off the bed and took a few steps out, then turned around. Her legs trembled, knees on the verge of buckling.

"Look. At. Me," he said with precision.

She lifted her chin and looked directly at the man with wide eyes.

"Say my name."

"Kenneth."

"Louder."

"Kenneth."

"Louder!" he screamed at the top of his lungs.

"Kenneth, my leader!" Anna cried.

She repeated "my leader" six or seven times, each one louder and more unhinged than the last.

Finally, he held up his palm. "And you will follow every one of my commands, right?"

"Yes, anything you say."

"Good. Now, I'll say it again, and I promise it will be the last time. Put on this dress," he said, never letting his eyes off her.

After wiping away the tears, Anna unbuttoned her dress and let it fall to the floor.

ONE

After leaving Motel 6, Hannah and Mark drove to downtown Laramie. They parked and walked until they came upon a neon sign flashing "The Dive." A flyer taped to the door read "Sunday Funday – $5 Bud Light Pitchers and $3 Wild Turkey shots."

"Look at that, it must be our lucky day. What do you say?" Mark said, gesturing to the door.

"With a name as horrible as The Dive, it must be a good place to get drunk," Hannah said.

The bar was packed, probably exceeding maximum capacity. Almost everyone seemed to be a student at the University of Wyoming. Some of the girls looked like they were barely eighteen, let alone twenty-one. Fake IDs had to be a booming business in Laramie, Hannah thought.

The scent of stale beer lingered in the air, and the floor was sticky, like walking over an insect trap. Cowboy hats hung on the wall, and dollar bills were stapled to the ceiling. Hannah was unsure of the significance of the dollars, maybe some sort of rite of passage for locals.

They squeezed through the crowd and sat at a high-top at the back of the bar. Some minutes later, a waitress approached their table, notepad in hand.

"What can I get you guys," she shouted over the crowd.

Mark ordered a pitcher and a round of Wild Turkey shots.

"Might as well make it two rounds," Hannah said, shrugging. "Saves you from making a second trip."

Since they'd stepped foot in the bar, country music had blared from the jukebox, and aside from Garth Brooks and Johnny Cash, she didn't recognize any of the other songs. Country was by far her least favorite genre, and outside of a few artists, she'd rather sit in silence. For a moment she considered picking Slayer or Pantera, but she decided against it, not wanting to incite a riot.

The waitress dropped off the drinks, and Mark slid a shot glass toward Hannah.

"Cheers," Mark said.

"Wait a minute, what are we cheersing to?"

Mark held the glass in the air, stroking his chin. "How about to the lovely state of Wyoming?"

They clanked their glasses together, and both took the shot without wincing.

"Now that the first drink is out of the way, I guess we should get to know each other. You go first, Hannah said.

"Let's see, where to start?" Mark said, glancing to the dollar-bill ceiling.

Mark was from Boston, it turned out, more specifically Cambridge—born in 1974, within two weeks of Hannah. His father was a cardiologist and his mother a librarian at MIT. Only one sibling, a younger sister in the third year of a pediatric residency program. Two years ago, Mark had graduated with a BS in Journalism from Boston University.

"My father thinks he's clever and likes to refer to it as a bullshit degree."

"So, I take it he doesn't want you to be a writer?"

Mark howled, drowning out the crowd and music for a moment.

"That's funny. He thinks any profession other than a doctor, lawyer, or architect is a waste of my time and his money. Since I was like four, my parents told me I was destined to be a cardiologist just like my father, but I've always been pretty squeamish around blood, so I knew that was never going to work out. Don't even get me started on needles either."

"Okay, let me do a quick recap," Hannah said, tapping her thumb on the table. "You're from a very successful and upper-class family living in New England, and your parents probably lie to their friends at parties about you and your career path."

"That pretty much sums it up."

"What you haven't said is what you're doing in Wyoming."

"I came out here to write the next great American Western."

"How is that coming?"

He took a sip. "To quote Donald Sutherland from *Animal House*, 'It's a piece of shit.'"

Hannah chuckled. "Seriously?"

"Let's just say, not as well as I planned. Occasionally, I have amazing inspiration, but most of the time I'll just stare at a blank screen for hours. I don't know, maybe I'm not cut out to be a writer. Maybe my father is right and I should just give up on my dream and go to fucking law school."

"No, please don't. The world doesn't need another lawyer." Hannah took a drink. "Wait a second, you're a trust fund baby, aren't you? No job. No worries about money. Traveling across the country pursuing your dream."

"I wouldn't say that. My parents cut me off about a year ago, and I had to sell my car. It was a '96 BMW 3 Series, my graduation present. I loved that car." He let out a deep sigh. "Now I have some clunker with almost 200,000 miles, and I've been living off the proceeds of the BMW ever since. Man, my dad blew his lid when I told him I sold the car."

The waitress stopped at the table, and Hannah ordered another pitcher.

"Are you trying to get me drunk, Hannah?"

She took the final sips of her beer. "I'm just trying to grease the wheel and get past all the stupid conversation people worry about on a first date."

"Oh, is that what you call this? A first date?"

Hannah rolled her eyes. "I think you've left out one major detail of your life."

"And that is?" Mark said, circling his index finger.

"If you're from Boston, where is that lovely New England accent?"

"Trust me, I've practiced long and hard to get rid of it, but give me a couple more of these and it'll slip out like a bride out of her dress on her wedding night," Mark said, holding up an empty shot glass.

"Awesome, I always wanted to have a conversation with someone who sounds exactly like Matt Damon."

"Not funny, Hannah, not in the slightest," Mark said, trying not to smile. "Okay, enough about me. It's your turn to spill the beans."

"I don't talk about myself to strangers," Hannah said with a smirk.

"No, no, no," he said, emphasizing the final one. "You made me tell you about my boring life, so you're not getting out of this that easy."

"Fine. My parents got divorced when I was sixteen. My father is a recovering alcoholic who's in remission from prostate cancer, and Margaret, the woman who gave birth to me, abandoned us. I haven't said more than a few words to her in years. She remarried this lawyer who has his face plastered on billboards all over Denver. I'm sure they probably run into your parents at rich people ski getaways in Aspen."

"Margaret? You don't call her your mother?"

"Nope. I stopped using that term years ago."

"Interesting."

"What does that mean?" Hannah said, eyebrows raised.

"Nothing, I'm just adding some commentary. What about siblings?"

"One sister, Casey, but she was murdered when she was a student at UW. She lived a few miles from here."

Hannah prepared herself for the customary response of "Oh my god" or "I'm so sorry" that she'd heard countless times.

"Fuck, I'm so sorry."

Hannah faked a smile, then told him about some of her work as a PI, the Megan Floyd case, and her investigation in Laramie that had solved Casey's murder. She intentionally left out that she'd nearly been killed by a serial killer.

"Jesus. I'm kind of at a loss for words."

"You don't have to say anything, I'd actually prefer if you didn't," Hannah said, searching for the waitress. Unable to locate her, Hannah turned back to Mark. "Sorry, but can we talk about something else?"

"Yes, of course."

For the next hour, the conversation was mindless. Favorite bands, best concert, dream vacation, and favorite food. They also continued ordering drinks, and Hannah lost count as her speech grew slurred.

During the chorus of "Friends in Low Places" by Garth Brooks, with nearly the entire bar singing along, Hannah leaned in and kissed Mark for the first time.

"What took you so long?" he asked.

"Do you want to go on an adventure with me?" Hannah said, stringing the words together. The spontaneity gave her an uneasy feeling, making her second-guess the proposal.

Without hesitation, he said, "What do you have in mind?"

"We get in the car and drive west. Stop when we want to stop, sleep when we get tired, eat at greasy diners, go to all the cheesy tourist spots that retirees live for, like the biggest ball of twine or random ghost towns. We'll hike, get drunk, fuck. Spend the next month or two living without a care in the world."

"Is this something that sounds like a great idea because you're drunk, but when you wake up, you'll pretend like you don't remember this conversation?"

"I'm dead serious. I'm leaving tomorrow morning, with or without you."

"You're not joking, are you?"

Hannah rolled her eyes. "What did I just say?"

"Sorry, I'm somewhat drunk and it's loud as fuck in here, so I'm a little befuddled. What do I do about my car?"

"I don't know. Park it at the bus station. Or the college. It'll be fine for a few months."

"And what if it gets towed? That's like $50 a day in an impound yard."

"You're worried about what you referred to as a clunker? What did it cost you? Like $500? A thousand?"

"It's got sentimental value."

"Well, if it gets towed, I'll pay to get it out or buy you another piece-of-shit car. Whatever is cheaper."

"You're really serious about this?"

Hannah let out a long sigh. "How drunk are you? I've already said I was serious."

"I'm just making sure, because you've only known me for all of—let's see," he said, raising his arm to pull back his sleeve and reveal his watch. "Exactly five hours. What if I'm some kind of psychopath? I mean I'm not, but you don't know that."

"You look like you're more of a guy who cries at commercials. And you definitely can't be any worse than what I've gone through the last few weeks."

Mark sipped his beer, then said, "Okay, let's do it. I do have to tell you something though."

"What?"

"I hate to be the bearer of bad news, but if your plan is to go west, you're not going to be able to see the biggest ball of twine. I believe that's in Nebraska. Maybe Kansas."

Hannah smiled, then took the final swig of her beer. "Well fuck, maybe we can visit the biggest thermometer instead."

"I'll do some research. I'm sure I can find some good stuff," he said. The New England accent finally slipped out.

"There it is! I've been waiting all night for it," Hannah said, laughing.

Sunlight pierced through the shades as Hannah rolled over on the hard mattress. She wiped the sleep out of her eyes and surveyed the room. She was alone, groggy, and hungover. Her head pounded with every slight movement.

The previous night was fuzzy, and the more she tried to remember, the more cracks started to open. She remembered going to the Cowboy Lounge, having drinks with Mark, kissing him and asking him to go on an adventure, but that was where her memories stopped. She didn't remember leaving the bar, or how she got back to the motel, or even climbing into bed.

She had no idea if he'd gone back to his room or if they had sex. It wouldn't have been the first time she'd slept with someone while blacked out.

In one swift motion, she pulled back the sheets and glanced down. She was still wearing her clothes from last night, minus her shoes and socks. Maybe he'd reconsidered her proposal and slipped out in the middle of the night.

The blackouts always worried Hannah. Not remembering what she did or said, or how she acted. Having to piece together the previous night like a puzzle.

Just as she was about to crawl out of bed, the door flew open. Mark stood in the doorway with a paper bag in hand.

"I hope you like sausage," he said, tossing a burrito on the mattress.

Hannah exhaled a sigh of relief. "I prefer bacon, but I guess this will do for now."

He smiled. "Eat up, it'll help that hangover."

"How do you know I have a hangover?" Hannah said, unwrapping the burrito.

Mark raised his eyebrows. "Are you being serious?"

"Was I that bad?"

"Let's just say I think you drank more than most of those college boys."

"I tend to do that sometimes," Hannah said, letting her embarrassment show. "I don't really remember leaving the bar."

"Let's see, we grabbed a cab, then when we got back here, you said you wanted a Jack and Coke, so I walked down to the vending machine, and when I got back, you were passed out."

"Stop."

Mark laughed. "I'm serious. You were sleeping lengthwise across the bed, so I took off your shoes and socks, then got you under the covers."

"Sorry, I'm sure your ideal first date doesn't involve having to take care of some drunk girl."

"Don't feel bad. I mean, you didn't throw up in my lap, so you're not even in the running for my worst first date ever."

"That's good." Hannah smiled. "I must've been really out, though, because I didn't even hear you leave this morning."

"Your snoring woke me up, so I decided to get my car and park it at the bus station. Then I headed back here, and I grabbed the burritos along the way."

"I think you've mistaken me for someone else, because I don't snore."

"Sorry to break it to you, but I'm pretty sure the people three rooms down could hear you."

Hannah rolled her eyes and tossed a pillow at him. He took a step back to avoid it.

"No sudden movements for the foreseeable future," she said, rubbing her eyes, her head throbbing.

"Nothing that a greasy burrito and a few glasses of water won't fix."

"God, I feel like such a lush. I'm sorry."

"You were fine, I promise. I think you passed out before you got to the really annoying stage."

"I'm glad to hear that," Hannah said, rolling her eyes again.

He smiled. "I did have one question about last night. Do you remember talking about going on an adventure?"

"I do remember."

"Were you being serious?"

Hannah nodded, taking a bite of the burrito.

"Perfect, Let's finish breakfast, then get the fuck out of here," he said.

Within the hour, they were driving west on I-80 with no real destination. All she wanted was to get far away from Laramie and her memories there. The farther they traveled, the more she felt that her life was returning to normal.

Over the next few weeks, they drove through parts of Wyoming and Utah that she'd had no idea existed, eating at gas stations, getting beers at roadside bars, having lunch at rest area picnic tables, stopping at every point of interest and scenic overlook. They took a picture at every state line and had lengthy conversations with the workers at the visitor centers.

So many towns they drove through that she'd never heard of. Rock Springs, Vernal, Castle Gate, Green River, Hanksville. Some were dying or already dead. Empty storefronts, decrepit buildings, boarded up windows, and very few people. For long stretches there wasn't a single other car in sight, and scattered across the countryside she saw more churches than homes.

They'd drive until they got tired or boredom kicked in. Then they'd stop at the nearest town, get a cheap room, get drunk, and have sex until they passed out. Sometimes they wouldn't leave the room for days. Their largest disagreement was pizza toppings, with Mark always wanting ham and pineapple and Hannah insisting pepperoni was the only acceptable choice. In the end, every pizza delivered arrived with one topping: pepperoni.

At a sporting goods store in Vernal, they purchased a tent, two sleeping bags, and a few hundred dollars of camping gear. They started switching where they slept. Some nights in the comfort of a hotel, and other nights camping anywhere they could find—state and national parks, BLM land, and even a few nights on private property. Hannah had been certain she'd hate camping, but she enjoyed it more than the hotel rooms. The wildlife, the forest, the solitude, and the notion there might not be another person for miles.

While they were exploring Torey, Utah, a local recommended they visit Cathedral Valley in Capital Reef National Park. The valley was twenty miles into a remote region of the park, only accessible by a dirt road that required a four-wheel drive and high ground clearance to navigate.

As they made their slow way along the road, all Hannah could think about was what if they had car issues? Running out of gas, a flat tire, high centering, anything that would leave them stranded. She recalled a German family of four who'd visited Death Valley, and similarly done an off-road trail in a rented minivan, but along the drive they got three flat tires and were never seen again. The minivan was discovered months later, but the tourists had never been found. The longer she thought about that family, the more anxious she became.

Anxiety was always in the back of her head, something she blamed on her dramatic childhood experiences. Some people were glass half full and some people were glass half empty. Hannah was glass shattered into hundreds of shards on the floor.

"Here, take a couple of these," Mark said, reaching

into his pocket. He opened his hand, and in his palm was a Ziploc baggy with several mushroom stems and caps.

"Where the fuck did you get those?"

"The kid at the liquor store from a few nights ago. I was saving them for a special occasion, and this seems as good as any."

"Do you think you should be eating these while you're driving?" Hannah said.

"I don't think I'm going to get pulled over out here. Anyways, it'll make this fucking drive a little more entertaining. Like playing a video game."

Hannah laughed, then ate two caps, nearly gagging on the last swallow.

To her surprise, the mushrooms eased her nerves, and for the rest of the drive, she stared out the window, fixated on a mountain on the horizon.

About an hour later, they arrived at the camp site, and after unloading the car, they set up their tent, started a fire, and grilled some hot dogs for dinner.

Later that night, they sat fireside, feet mere inches from the crackling flames. As Mark was reading *The Great Gatsby* to her, there was a howl Hannah had never heard before. It sent a shiver of fear throughout her entire body.

She shot upright. "Umm, what the fuck was that?"

Mark turned his head, then took a small sip of whiskey. "I think some of the Manson family migrated out here after Charlie got locked up."

She smacked his shoulder. "Shut up, I'm being serious. What was it?"

Hannah scanned the land, but trying to see beyond the campfire was futile, like staring into the abyss.

"Calm down. It's just a pack of coyotes, maybe two. And by the sounds of it, they're at least a few miles away.

Geez, you look freaked out. Have you never been camping before?"

"Yes, once or twice when I was like twelve. Are you sure it's coyotes?"

"Yes, I'm positive. Once you hear that howl, you'll never forget it."

"And you know this for a fact? Were you a Boy Scout or some shit?"

"An Eagle Scout, actually."

For a moment Hannah forgot the screams as she burst out laughing. "You were an Eagle Scout?"

"Yes, and I'm very proud of that accomplishment. And you shouldn't make fun, because I can start a fire using just friction, and can tie nearly every knot known to man, and can navigate using only a compass. I think you should be thankful you have such a well-versed outdoorsman with you in this setting."

"I'm not making fun. I just wouldn't have put that on my bingo card of things you were going to tell me tonight. I guess there's so much I don't know about you," she said staring up to the night sky.

The more time she spent under the stars, the more Hannah grew to like, then eventually love it. She daydreamed about buying a remote piece of land, somewhere in Colorado west of the Continental Divide. Build a small cabin. Nothing extravagant. A bedroom, bathroom, and small kitchen. That was all she'd need.

Sometimes those daydreams included Mark, sometimes they didn't. She was fine with the ones that didn't include him. It'd be her, and a couple of cats, a dog and some livestock. Live life away from cities, away from traffic, and people.

He took another sip. "I'm an open book."

Hannah leaned over and kissed him. "Not tonight, I'm

exhausted. I'm going to bed."

When Hannah awoke, Mark wasn't in the tent. She was about to call to him, but decided not to, wanting to be alone. Since she'd been with him, the only times she'd had to herself were when one of them was in the bathroom.

After wiping the sleep out of her eyes, she watched the shadows dance on the tent's roof. As much as she loved time with Mark, Hannah was an introvert. She preferred being alone most days, so spending almost every waking moment with someone was difficult.

But there was also something else that lived in her head—that their time together was too good to be true. It was those dark thoughts that she was always fighting.

That if he ever knew who she truly was, if she ever shared her darkest secrets, and what she thought about in the middle of the night when she couldn't sleep, he'd run and never come back. Those dark thoughts were never far. Always telling her that he had ulterior motives. That he was using her. That he was going to hurt her. That he was going to break her heart.

"Come on, you need to see this sunrise," Mark said, climbing into the tent with a cup of coffee.

Hannah took a sip. "This tastes like shit," she said.

"Sorry, it's the best I can do without access to my espresso machine. Now get up and let's go before we miss it."

They started out east as the sun began to break on the horizon. They walked in utter silence, the only sounds coming from their footsteps crunching on the barren desert floor. In their path was a dry vista and a series of sandstone monoliths stretching to the sky. Millions of years of erosion, exposing layers of red, orange, and yellow. Formations that began before any human, and would continue to erode long after their extinction.

Hannah wandered about thirty feet off the trail, then stopped and looked down at the ground below her boots. She kicked up some dirt and had a strange feeling that no human had ever stood in that exact spot. Maybe it was true, or maybe it was part of the residual psychedelic effects of the mushrooms.

A lizard peeked its head out from behind a yucca, stared at them, and then turned and scurried away.

"That's Temple of the Sun," Mark whispered, pointing to the monolith directly in front of them.

They stopped and watched the sun break over the crest of the peak.

After some time, Hannah turned back and looked over her shoulder. The camp, the car, the smoke from the fire, all gone. No signs of human activity besides their footprints in the sand. It was like they had stepped into a portal and been transported to another planet.

"I've never seen anything so beautiful," she said.

Mark smiled and wrapped his arms around her and kissed her neck. At that moment, they could've been the only people alive, and she would've been content with that.

After leaving Capital Reef, they made their way to St. George, then south on I-15 toward California and the Pacific Ocean. Both of them were exhausted from driving, so they decided to take a detour and spend a few nights in Las Vegas.

When they checked into Caesars Palace, Hannah mentioned it was her first time in the city, so the hotel clerk upgraded them to a suite on the fifteenth floor. They navigated to the room, and as Mark sat on the bed, Hannah stared out the window overlooking the Strip.

"Since it's your first time here, you pick what we do first," Mark said, bouncing on the mattress.

"All I know is I need a drink."

For the next two days, they walked the Strip more times than they could count, always with a drink in hand. Hannah wanted to play blackjack, but she was anxious that she'd play the wrong hand, and everyone at the table would yell at her, so she stuck to nickel slots, winning $100. They ate every meal at a buffet and got half-price tickets to Siegfried & Roy, which they both found underwhelming.

As sunrise broke on their last night, Hannah and Mark gazed out of their hotel window. The street was nearly deserted, except for a few degenerate gamblers looking for a last jackpot before breakfast.

"What do you think about getting married?" Mark said, his words sticky.

"Just the concept of marriage, or me and you?" Hannah said, glancing at him.

"You and me. I think Hannah Foster has a nice ring to it."

"I think you've had a little too much to drink."

"That I can't dispute, but what do you say? Haven't you ever wanted to get married?"

Hannah snorted, then chugged the rest of her drink. "God no."

"So, you never want to get married? You're going to be some seventy-five-year-old lady with a dozen cats, aren't you?"

"Oh, I'm not going to live that long."

"No?"

Hannah shook her head. "I already have a plan."

"A plan, huh?"

"Yes, I'm still figuring out the exact age, but somewhere between sixty-five and, say, seventy, I'm going to rent a car, get really fucking drunk, and drive into the Grand Canyon."

Mark looked at her for a long, silent stretch. "Can I reserve a spot in the trunk?"

"I think I can accommodate that," Hannah said.

They shared a laugh, and Mark squeezed her hand.

"There are probably over a hundred chapels within a twenty-block radius down there. It's easy. We go to the courthouse, get a marriage license, then go to one of the chapels and have an Elvis impersonator marry us. I bet we can do the whole thing in under an hour. We'll be back before the breakfast buffet closes."

Hannah bit her bottom lip, holding back the urge to burst out laughing. "You want to get married by Elvis? Are you serious?"

"Are you not an Elvis fan? I guess I should've asked. I bet we could find someone else to do it. Maybe a magician? How does a little magic mixed into the ceremony sound?"

Hannah rolled her eyes. "No, I mean are you serious about getting married?"

"Yeah, why not?"

"How long has it been since we left Laramie? A month?"

"On Tuesday it'll be six weeks."

"And you want to marry me? I may be mistaken, and maybe it occurred when I was blackout drunk, but we haven't even said 'I love you' to each other."

"I love you. See, it's not that hard. Now you give it a try," Mark said.

"That easy, huh?"

"I pretty much fell in love with you the first night we hung out, but I didn't say it because I didn't want to freak you the fuck out."

Hearing Mark tell him he loved her gave Hannah mixed feelings. A part of her wanted to kiss him and say yes to the proposal, but her cynical side was terrified of commitment. That side had a habit of sabotaging relationships, and it almost always won.

Hannah snatched Mark's drink and finished it in three gulps. "Let's say we do it. Then what?"

Mark took the empty cup back from her. "I haven't thought that far ahead."

"You do realize at some point we'll have to return to a normal life. I'll go back to Denver, and the agency. And who knows where you'll end up."

"Denver sounds nice," Mark said.

"Have you ever been?"

"No, but I've seen pictures and it seems lovely." He tossed the cup on the bed, then took her hand again. "So, are you turning down my proposal?"

Hannah rested her forehead against the window and stared down at the pool. Even though she knew the glass was at least a few inches thick, and probably could withstand tornado-force winds, she couldn't stop thinking about falling through and tumbling to the pavement.

After a few seconds, she muttered, "I don't know if it's the smartest idea for either of us."

"And why not? I don't think I've ever had more fun with another person in my life. We've never had a fight, barely a disagreement. And just so you know, I'm willing to concede about the pizza toppings."

"That's because we've been on an extended vacation. We've been getting drunk, and traveling to some of the most amazing spots in the country, and eating whatever we want, and fucking like rabbits. What could we possibly fight about?"

Mark glanced at the ceiling. "That is a valid point."

"Can we talk about this again when we're not

completely wasted?" Hannah said, praying he'd never broach the subject again.

He nodded.

"Oh, come on, I don't want to see a frown on that pretty face."

Hannah squeezed Mark's hand and led him to the bed, then pushed him down onto the mattress. After unzipping her pants, she wiggled out of them and kicked them across the room.

Sometime later that morning, Hannah awoke gasping for air. She sprang up and tried to swallow but couldn't. It felt as if she were drowning. She ran to the bathroom, turned on the faucet, and began splashing water into her mouth. After about ten handfuls, her breathing returned to normal.

At first, she thought it was caused by heartburn from the three oversized Margaritas she'd downed, but then she remembered a similar episode shortly after Casey's murder, and an adolescent psychiatrist chalking it up to a severe anxiety attack. The start of her short-lived SSRI journey.

Without making a sound, Hannah crawled back into bed and sat completely still for a long time, watching Mark sleep. As tears rolled down her cheeks, she wiped them away, deciding their days together were numbered.

One week later, they were sitting on Santa Monica beach with their feet in the sand, moonlight shining down, and waves rhythmically crashing into the shore, coming closer and closer. High tide was rolling in.

Marriage had not come up again, and since leaving Las Vegas, there seemed to be a division between them.

Their carefree, happy-go-lucky attitudes had shifted into something more common to a traditional couple. Hannah hated the new dynamic, and she was certain Mark felt the same.

She began to convince herself that they were too different. The two worlds they came from were always constant in her thoughts, and that would slowly erode their relationship, eventually turning it into something that couldn't be repaired.

He preferred the Beatles over Pink Floyd. He had an education from a prestigious college, and she'd barely graduated from high school. He came from a well-respected family, and she was the poster child of a dysfunctional one.

The more she thought about their future, the more she convinced herself it was time to run. When she ran, she didn't have to worry about disappointment, or the fear of not being loved, or the fear of losing someone like Casey again.

"Do you wanna hear something I've never told anyone before?" Hannah said, digging her toes in the sand.

She wasn't sure why she was telling Mark the story. Maybe it was the sound of the ocean, and the warmth of his body next to hers, and the fear of what tomorrow would bring.

"I do," Mark said, sitting up.

Hannah stared out at the water for nearly a minute, watching the waves roll back into the sea.

"When I was ten, I went with Casey to my grandma's down in Orlando for a couple weeks during summer break. She had this timeshare in Palm Coast that we'd spend a few days at it whenever we were down there. It was this amazing little bungalow that was like two blocks from the beach, so we'd walk to the ocean every day. Play in the water, make sand castles, eat corn dogs. Stupid kid shit. God, I used to love those concession stand corn dogs. It must have something to do with the perfect combination of grease, and oil, and who knows what else."

"You've never told me about your love of corn dogs. Are you telling me we could've been eating them this entire time?"

Hannah glared at him. "Can I continue?"

"Sorry, trying to make a joke. Yes, please go on."

"Well, on our last day, we went down to the ocean one more time. After a few hours, Casey and my grandma went to grab something to eat, and I was just walking along the shoreline. I must've been distracted or something, but a rip current hit and before I could react, I was upside down, underwater and being pulled out to sea. By the time I got my head above water, I was at least a hundred feet out. My head was bobbing in and out, and I could barely see the shore, and every time I tried to scream, my mouth filled with water."

Hannah kicked up some sand and took a deep breath.

"I knew how to swim, but I was a kid, and the more I tried to get back to shore, the farther it pulled me out. It was so strong, and I was getting so tired, and looking back at it now, I think I was coming to the realization that I was going to drown. Well, I was about to give up, but then I felt someone grab my arm, and before I knew it, I was on some man's back. I don't think I've ever held on to someone so tight. I'm surprised I didn't strangle him."

Hannah let out a shaky laugh. "It felt like it took forever to make it back to shore, but once my feet were in the sand, I dropped to my knees and started bawling. By then a small crowd had formed, and at some point, Casey and my grandma ran up and began hugging me. It was all such a blur. Well, in all the confusion, the man who saved me slipped out of the crowd, and I never got to thank him. Fuck, I never even got his name.”

“And you never found him?”

“Nope. He vanished like a ghost.” She closed her eyes and could almost see the crowd as vivid as that day. “Now that I think about it, I don’t think anyone knows that I almost drowned. I mean, all the bystanders do, but they don’t know me, and probably forgot about it an hour later, like driving by an accident. And Casey and my grandma are dead.”

Mark wrapped his arms around her and they sat in the sand, listening to the crashing waves.

As the water washed over their feet, Hannah whispered, “To this day, I’m still terrified of the fucking ocean.”

That night, she slipped out of bed and grabbed her backpack, which she’d already filled with her belongings when Mark passed out. Motionless, Hannah watched him sleep. Deep breaths and drool rolling down his chin and onto the pillow. She smiled. She was going to miss him.

For a minute or so, she fought herself. She almost dropped the backpack and crawled back into bed, but she knew the relationship had run its course. Maybe in some other world, some other life, some other universe, she could be happy, but not in this one.

“Mark,” she whispered, tapping his shoulder.

He didn’t move. Hannah whispered two more times, each one louder.

“What’s up babe?” he said, his breath reeking of whiskey.

“I’m leaving. I’m going back home.”

He stared at her, probably trying to decipher if he was

dreaming. Finally, he said, "You're going where?"

"Home. Denver," Hannah said, her voice so thin it almost cracked.

Mark sat up. "The both of us, or are you going alone?"

"I'm going alone."

He started rubbing his eyes. "What's going on, Hannah? Did I do something?"

"No, I promise. There are a few things I need to do regarding the Terry Stone case that I can't put off any longer."

"I'll go with you. Give me ten minutes and I'll be ready."

All she wanted was for him to stop talking, because the more she heard his voice, the greater the odds were she'd reconsider her decision.

She turned away. "No, I think it's best you stay here. I've paid for the room until the end of the week, and that envelope on the table has $2,500 in it. That should be enough to get you to Laramie and get your car back."

"Please don't do this Hannah," Mark said.

Swallowing hard, she said, "It's already done."

When Hannah arrived at the duplex of Denise Long's mother, she remained in her car for a while, rehearsing the first few sentences she would say. Over and over and over again, like she was preparing for a play.

Outside on the doorstep, she ran over her lines one final time, then knocked on the wooden screen door. Peering through the screen, Hannah could see the back of a Lazy-Boy rocking in the middle of the living room. *The Price Is Right* was on at a volume Hannah could hear about halfway up the sidewalk.

Knowing knocking was pointless, Hannah leaned into

the door and called out through the mesh screen, "Mrs. Long!"

Hannah repeated it three more times until the chair stopped moving. "Hold your horses, I'm coming," a voice yelled over the TV.

A frail woman, aged well beyond her years, trudged down the hallway. At the door, she leaned heavily on a cane with one hand. The other was strategically placed on her hip, elbow out, seemingly to maintain balance.

"Did you find Cleo?" she said in a rough voice. Years of smoking had probably destroyed her vocal cords.

"Cleo? I'm sorry, I don't know who that is."

"It's the building cat. She disappeared a few weeks ago, and we don't know if she found a new home or if something happened to her."

"No, sorry, I didn't find Cleo."

The woman glared at Hannah, and for a moment it seemed like she was going to slam the door. "Are you selling something? You better not have gotten me away from my shows to try to sell me something that I can't afford."

"No, I'm not a solicitor. I'm looking for Mary Long," Hannah said, stumbling over her words. The topic of Cleo had thrown a curve-ball into the lines she'd practiced.

"I'm Mary."

"I'm sorry to show up unannounced, but I didn't want to call. Umm, my name is Hannah Jacobs and I'm a private investigator from Denver. I have an update about your daughter's case."

Before driving to Mary's duplex, Hannah had visited the parents of Diana Allen in Greeley. When Hannah told them she was a PI and had information on Diana's murder, they slammed the door in her face.

"Leave us the fuck alone! Diana is at peace, and if you

don't get off our property, we'll call the police!" the man had yelled from the other side of the door.

It seemed they'd come to terms with the murder and didn't want to reopen old wounds.

Alice Sander's parents were dead—her father of a heart attack and her mother of breast cancer six months later. Judy Meyers's parents had moved to the Florida Keys. Julia Boone's father had died in a car crash shortly after her murder, his BAC three times the legal limit, and her mother had disappeared, her whereabouts unknown. That left Mary as the only parent of one of the murdered girls still alive and living in the region.

Mary took a while. Finally, she said, "Come in."

She ushered Hannah to the two-chair Formica kitchen table set. Hannah had to contort her legs to fit behind the table. After fetching two glasses of tea, Mary took a careful seat across from Hannah. Her breathing was labored, maybe COPD or emphysema.

"I never imagined a pretty thing like you would show up on my doorstep with news about my baby. If I'm being honest, I actually didn't think I'd hear anything about Denise's case ever again. I bet it's been at least three years since anyone from that worthless police department called me. At the beginning, I talked to one of the investigators almost every week—I think his name was Fisher or something—but the longer the case went on, the more I pestered him, and the less he returned my calls, until he just flat out stopped."

"And you're the next contestant on *The Price Is Right*," the TV blared from the living room.

Mary looked away for a moment, then took a sip and turned back to Hannah. "Lay it on me, sweetie, and you don't have to beat around the bush. I had to identify her at the morgue, so I'm prepared for anything you have to say."

"Did you see the news about what happened in Laramie a few months back?"

"No. After Denise, I stopped watching the news, reading the paper, pretty much anything that deals with current events. It's all death and destruction. Bombings in the Middle East, people getting stabbed in the streets, murder this, killing that. Nope. I've had enough heartbreak in my life. I don't need to seek it out in my free time."

Hannah let out a long sigh. "I'm almost positive I found the man who killed Denise. He killed my sister as well, and I believe there were at least another four victims, maybe five."

Hannah explained the similarities between all the victims, noting how nearly every murder shared the same MO. All Caucasian females under thirty with short, brunette hair. All of them were single and living alone, and all but one of the murders had happened at night, on a waning crescent moon, at the victim's apartment. The method of murder was either strangulation or stabbing. And then the most significant piece of evidence, to Hannah at least. The jewelry she'd found in Terry's house.

Hannah lifted her necklace, dangling it in front of Mary.

"My sister wore this necklace every day, and when she was murdered, the necklace vanished. Last December, I broke into a man's house, the man I suspected was the killer, and found it, along with six other pieces of jewelry. One of them, I believe, was Denise's."

Hannah lowered the necklace and slipped it under her shirt.

"You have something from Denise?" Mary said, holding back tears.

"No. There was an explosion, and all the other jewelry is gone, along with that man."

"The man who murdered her is dead?"

Hannah nodded.

"Who was he?"

"Terry Stone. Born in '59, and lived most of his life in Laramie. He went to high school there, and was a sophomore at the University of Wyoming, majoring in wildlife biology when a truck driver ran a red light and T-boned his car. When paramedics arrived, they stated chances of survival were slim."

Mary removed a handkerchief and wiped her nose. "If that truck driver would've killed this man, he would've never gotten his hands on my Denise."

Hannah nodded gravely. That was something she'd thought about countless times. If that truck driver had been going a little faster, or been a few seconds earlier, Terry might've died that day, and those women would've never been murdered, and those families, her family, would've never been destroyed.

Hannah continued. "He was in a coma for the next eight months, and after he regained consciousness, he spent another six months in the hospital. About a year after he was released, he was awarded a little over a million dollars for the crash. He purchased a house and a few acres outside of Laramie, dropped out of school, and never really held a regular job after that."

Hannah took a sip of tea and cleared her throat.

"For the next decade, he traveled all over Wyoming and throughout parts of Montana, South Dakota, and northern Colorado. The money from the settlement allowed him to go where ever he wanted. Then, in July of 1988, he returned to Laramie and most likely began stalking my sister, killing her in January of 1989."

Mary hung on every word, her fingers trembling over the table.

"I believe my sister was his first murder, then another girl two years later in Gillette. Then in the summer of '94, he appeared in Rapid City. I was able to obtain his credit card records, and he got a room about ten blocks from Denise's apartment, at the Horseshoe Motel."

"I've driven by there hundreds of times," Mary said.

"I spoke to the owner, and he keeps very detailed records of every guest. Well, after doing a little persuading, he located a receipt and a photocopy of Terry's driver's license."

Hannah slid the photocopy across the table. Mary fixated on Terry's face, her fingers tapping the bottom of the picture. Hannah waited about twenty seconds for her to say something. When Mary didn't, she continued, "He stayed there for ten nights, and on the ninth night, Denise was murdered."

"This is the bastard that killed my baby," Mary said, finally looking up.

"I believe so."

"Why her?"

"The why is the tougher question. I don't know for certain, but he definitely had a type. Denise and another victim, Julia Boone, looked like they could've been twins."

"You said six girls were murdered by this man?"

"Yes, five or six."

"How did no one discover this guy after the first murder, or the second, or the fucking third one?" Mary said, her voice unsteady.

"He was smart, very smart. He never left a single piece of evidence. No fingerprints, no blood, nothing. And I believe he had knowledge that small town police agencies don't have great communication, and that makes it very difficult to connect cases across state lines and even across counties. He also took cooling-off periods, spanning the murders out over years, making them seem like one-offs or crimes of passion. Hell, I always thought the person who killed my sister was someone she knew from school or work."

"So, since you're here, and not the police, I'm assuming he'll never be charged with Denise's murder?"

"I highly doubt it. He probably won't be charged in any of them. The sheriff in Laramie refused to prosecute a dead man."

Mary stared down on the table like she was trying to memorize the patterns. Without looking up, she placed her hands on Hannah's.

"The last time I talked to Denise, we got in a fight over forty dollars. Forty measly dollars. She was always borrowing twenty here, forty there. I mean, it felt like she was asking for money nearly every darn week. Well, I got tired of it and told her she needed to grow up, and that I couldn't keep giving her money. I just wanted her to learn some responsibility, because I knew I wouldn't be around forever to help her out. I told her not to come back until she had a steady paycheck. I was just trying to teach her a lesson, you know. Nothing more."

"I understand," Hannah whispered.

"I think about that conversation every day. I told her not to come back, and she didn't. The last time I saw her, she was walking out that door, flipping me off. I still have nightmares about her leaving."

A picture frame hung in the living room, a collage inside it. Every picture was of Denise throughout the years. Elementary school, then high school graduation, and finally early adulthood.

"That is my sweet Denise. She was a little firecracker when she was a kid. She'd go from being half asleep to the loudest kid in the neighborhood. After her dad died, it was just me and her. We struggled a lot. I was bouncing checks left and right, and there was a stretch where we lived in my car."

"And I'm Bob Barker, reminding you to help control the pet population. Have your pet spayed or neutered," blared from the living room. Neither of them flinched.

"One time, after dropping her off at school, I overheard a group of kids making fun of her for being homeless, and she just smiled and walked away. She could've been a brat or a jerk, but she never complained. Not once. She always said, 'It's going to get better, Mom, I just know it.'" The woman paused and wiped away tears. "She was the rock, the strong one. I wouldn't have survived those years without her."

Mary covered her mouth and coughed. "I stopped drinking when she turned twelve, and I got a decent job at Safeway. I finally was able to get this place, and for a few years, life was really good. We still struggled, but we had each other to lean on, to get us through difficult situations. Then, she was gone, and I was utterly broken."

Hearing the despair in Mary's voice, Hannah couldn't help but to think if that was what she'd sound like in ten, twenty, thirty years. Always wondering what would've been if Casey were still alive. The thought of the murder always with her until she died, like a terminal disease.

"When I was making her arrangements, I barely had any money, and I sure as shit couldn't afford a headstone. All she got was a tiny ten-by-ten plaque with her name, birthday, and the day she died. That's all that marks her life." Mary tried to smile, but it looked more like a grimace. "I go out there twice a week and clean it, cut away the grass and rest a bouquet of flowers next to it." Her cadence slowed. "I'm worried once I pass, no one will clean it, and her name will begin to fade, until one day it's completely vanished."

For the first time in minutes, Mary looked at Hannah. "I'm so sorry, I've been rambling. Where are you from?"

"Colorado. Born in Fort Collins, but I've lived in Denver for the last twelve years," Hannah said, trying to remember if that really was the exact number.

"That's a long drive to come and tell me all this. I wish I could give you some money for gas or a motel or something, but I don't get paid until next week, so I'm a little tight at the moment."

"No, no, it's fine. If you tried to give me money, I wouldn't accept it."

Mary smiled. "The world would be a lot better off if there were more people like you."

They continued talking, mostly reminiscing about Denise and Casey.

"Were you close to her?" Mary said.

"Very much. She was my best friend. I'm still pretty lost without her."

She smiled again. "I hope someday you'll be at peace. Don't hold on to it forever, or you'll end up like me, and that is the last thing you want."

Almost an hour after Hannah sat down in the kitchen, Mary thanked her and offered her a handmade cinnamon roll. Hannah declined the offer, but Mary was persistent.

"Please, take two. Let me find you a Tupperware," Mary said, rummaging through drawers. "And you don't have to return it."

"They look delicious," Hannah said, staring at the pastries, which were as big as her hands.

Back in her car, Hannah grabbed her checkbook, wrote a check for $1,000, and added "For Denise's Headstone" in the memo line. She folded the check in half and slipped it into Mary's mailbox before driving away.

TWO

The phone rang, and Hannah stared at it half-heartedly, her head pounding after another long night of drinking. As she stared, she tried to piece the night together. She distinctly remembered going to a couple bars in Capital Hill but couldn't recall leaving or how she'd made it home.

Since returning from South Dakota, she'd been on a historic bender. Almost every night for a month, she drank to excess, blacking out about half the time. Work, get drunk, pass out, and wake up with very little memory of the previous night. Repeat, repeat, and repeat.

Hannah had thought her demons would vanish after solving Casey's murder, and for a brief period they did, especially when she was with Mark. But the moment she stepped foot back in Denver, they'd returned, as vocal as ever.

The phone rang a second time. Again, she stared at it, her head ringing twice as loud with each chime.

"Fuck off," she muttered, wanting to throw the phone across the room.

Hannah daydreamed about Mark often—more than she liked to admit. There were nights when she considered dropping everything and going back to California, but she knew the chances of finding him were slim to none. Where would she even start? And if she did find him, what would she say? She'd left him high and dry, with no reason other than she was scared.

And even if he did take her back, he'd probably have a constant, nagging reminder that she'd already left once. What would stop her from leaving again? Like taking someone back after they've cheated.

A third ring.

Their time together had been intense, like jamming years into months, the kind of months most couples strive for. It was a summer romance that felt like a fairy tale, and that was exactly what scared Hannah.

For as long as she could remember, she'd daydreamed about the kind of relationship she found with Mark, but then when she was actually in it, she'd felt uneasy. During the last few days with him, she'd felt claustrophobic, like everything was collapsing in on her.

Fourth ring.

Maybe Hannah was destined to be alone. Some people had soulmates, while others, possibly her, were never meant to. That was what she tried to convince herself of those nights she stared blankly at the ceiling at three in the morning, unable to sleep.

Mark had never asked about her scars, and why she made them, and what they meant, and if they hurt. He didn't judge them or her, and she loved him for that. She wished she would've told him.

Finally, she picked up the phone just as the fifth ring began.

"I'm sorry Hannah, I know you said you wanted to

be left alone until the afternoon, but there's a woman in the lobby insisting to see you. She said she knows you." It was Kimmy, Hannah's part-time assistant. She kept her voice quiet, likely aware that Hannah was suffering from another unbearable hangover.

"Who is it?" Hannah sighed.

"I asked three times, but she wouldn't tell me. I promise, I tried."

"What does she want?"

"Again, she won't tell me."

"Does she look crazy?"

There was a moment of silence. Then, as if cupping the receiver, Kimmy whispered, "Not in the slightest. She looks like she has money. Her dress looks like it cost more than my entire wardrobe. And she has a matching Versace handbag."

"Okay, send her in in about a minute."

Hannah hung up, then removed a bottle of Bayer from her top drawer and dry-swallowed two aspirin. She closed her eyes and began massaging her temples. Almost exactly sixty seconds later, the door opened, and the woman stepped into the office.

Without hesitation, Hannah said, "What the hell are you doing here, Margaret?"

"That's how you greet your mother? You know I don't like when you call me by my first name."

Hannah smirked. "Do you think I really care about what you like and don't like?" I hate your guts, and I could go the rest of my life without seeing you, she added in her head.

Countless times, Hannah had pondered how a mother could leave a daughter, pretending like they'd never been born. It was likely one of the reasons why Hannah had so many broken relationships and feared getting close to anyone. On the rare occasions she did, her instinct was to run. Pretty much everything Hannah hated about herself she could pinpoint back to Margaret.

Margaret frowned. "I don't like your tone, Hannah. It's very unpleasant. Very unladylike. I know I didn't raise you to talk in such a manner."

Hannah attempted to recall an endearing moment with the woman. A birthday, Christmas, a vacation? Nothing came to mind. *Was there actually not a single memory, or had she scrubbed everything regarding Margaret?*

"My father raised me, not you. And don't ever think anything else."

"Could you please just be cordial while I'm here?"

"And why exactly is that?"

For a moment, she thought Margaret might be dying, something terminal, and she was there to make amends with Hannah, but that notion quickly faded. Hannah was certain that Margaret would never apologize for leaving after Casey died, even on her deathbed.

Margaret looked around the office. Without her saying a word or even changing her expression, Hannah knew she was repulsed by the decor. Almost all the furniture had been purchased at Ikea, except for the blue-upholstered antique wingback chair that she'd bought at an estate sale. That was one of Hannah's most prized possessions.

She'd purchased the chair from a cheery lady named Gretchen. Gretchen was selling most of her belongings and returning home to England after living in Colorado for almost three decades. She wanted to give Hannah a discount because she said Hannah had kind eyes. Hannah refused, but Gretchen was persistent, and after some back and forth, they agreed on $40.

Margaret was dressed as if she were going to a high-ticket charity event, and she smelled of a perfect floral combination that Hannah couldn't place. Most likely a scent Hannah could never afford. She wondered if Margaret had driven herself or if she had a driver downstairs waiting for her.

"Have you received my messages?" Margaret said.

Hannah nodded, tapping her thumb on the desk.

"And you couldn't bother to return my calls?"

"No, just like I never respond to your letters, or if you projected the bat signal into the sky, I wouldn't respond to that either. What else do I need to do to convey that I don't want anything to do with you?" Hannah shifted in her chair. She'd never directly told Margaret how she felt about her, and it felt liberating. "I thought we had an unspoken agreement. You pretend like I was never born, and I pretend like I don't have a mother."

Margaret stared at Hannah, barely blinking. Finally, she said, "Can I sit down?"

Hannah remained still for a few seconds, then gestured to the chair in front of the desk. Margaret eased into it and positioned her handbag symmetrically in her lap. In the back of her mind, Hannah was always concerned she'd run into her somewhere in the city, and thinking about what she would say, but she'd never expected Margaret to lower herself and set foot into her office.

"How long has it been since we've seen each other?" Four years?" Margaret said.

Hannah glared at her, exhaling out of her nostrils. Jaw locked, she slowly shook her head. "It's been eight years. It was when I took the train to Glenwood for Thanksgiving."

The vodka on Margaret's breath could've started a campfire. It wasn't even noon yet. The apple doesn't fall far from the tree. "Yes, that is right. That was a lovely trip."

Hannah's recollection wasn't as blissful. She'd been barely nineteen, and had accepted an invitation to spend

Thanksgiving with Margaret and her new husband, Steve, along with his two children, Emily and Ryan, both soon to be teenagers, at their mountain mansion in Glenwood Springs.

Hannah took the train, the Colorado Zephyr, from Union Station in Denver to Glenwood Springs. It was the first time she'd ever been on a train, and she gazed out the window in awe as it crossed the Continental Divide, and then made its way down to the Colorado River through Byer and Glenwood Canyon. Hannah was excited for the visit and the possibility of reconciling her relationship with Margaret, and forming one with her stepfather and stepsiblings.

Within an hour of arriving, Hannah knew the trip was a mistake. She felt like an outsider, like a charity case, like she didn't belong. She wondered if the invitation was a mistake, or made out of pity, and they'd secretly been hoping that Hannah wouldn't be gullible enough to accept.

Her room was in a different wing of the house, away from the other bedrooms, and probably intended for the housekeeper, or whatever help they had on the payroll. During meals, barely anyone talked to her, and she considered taking her plate and eating in her room alone.

On Friday morning, Margaret told Hannah that it was a family tradition to go skiing in Aspen on Black Friday, and since Hannah didn't know how to ski, she could either spend the day on the bunny slopes or stay at the house. She opted to stay at the house, where she used almost an entire box of Kleenex wiping away her tears.

She cursed herself for making the trip. If she had driven, she would have left that day and driven back to Denver. She strongly considered walking the five miles in twenty-something-degree weather to the train station but decided she was more likely to freeze to death than make it there.

On Saturday, the last night of the long weekend, a knock came on her door around midnight. Hannah was hesitant to answer, like fearing the call of a debt collector. After what felt like a minute, she finally got off the bed and opened the door.

"Can I come in?" Emily said in a thin voice.

Hannah peered into the hallway, making sure that she was alone, then gestured her inside.

Emily didn't say a word for the first few minutes, scanning the room like she'd never been in it before. Hannah was about to ask why she'd come when she finally spoke.

"Would you like to play cards with me?"

Hannah agreed, and as they played Uno, it was the only hint of normalcy she experienced during the entire trip. They talked about music, TV shows, and movies. Sometime that night, they snuck down to the kitchen and raided the pantry for Pop-Tarts and Oreos.

After devouring a strawberry Pop-Tart, Emily confided that her dream job was to be a screenwriter, and that she had written a couple small plays but was too terrified to share them with her parents or Ryan.

"Would you show me one?" Hannah asked.

"Umm, not tonight. I don't think they're ready just quite yet, but I promise the next time you visit, I'll show you."

Hannah smiled. "I can't wait," she said, knowing there would never be another visit.

A little before sunrise, they played the final hand, and as Emily was leaving the room, she stopped and turned back.

"I'm sorry about Mom and Dad. I feel like they were kind of jerks to you this weekend."

Hannah looked away and took a deep breath. "It's fine. I have a tumultuous relationship with Margaret, and obviously your father is going to side with her. I came up here with the hopes of fixing our relationship, but I don't think it worked very well."

Clearing her throat, Emily said, "Sometimes I feel like an outsider in this house, and this might sound pretty dumb, but I had more fun tonight with you than I've had with anyone in this family for a long time."

"It's not dumb at all," Hannah said.

"Get home safe, and hopefully we'll get to hang out soon."

For those few brief hours, Hannah felt like she had a sister again, and it had made her realize how much she missed Casey.

The following morning, Steve and Margaret dropped Hannah off at the train station. Neither of them stepped foot out of the car to assist with her luggage or wish her off. Barely looking in Hannah's direction, Margaret muttered, "It was nice seeing you." No "I love you." No "I'll miss you." No hug. Not a single sign of affection.

The last time Margaret had uttered the word "love" to Hannah was on the day of Casey's funeral, and since then, the closest words of endearment had been, "Take care, sweetie." Even saying those words had probably made her skin crawl.

Without veering back, Hannah boarded the train, vowing to herself that she'd never use the word "mom" or "mother" again, and that she'd exile Margaret from her life. It'd been years since she'd heard Margaret's shrill voice, and that wasn't long enough.

"You really need to come up again—we've done some amazing renovations. The house looks nothing like it did when you were there."

"I think I'll pass."

Margaret frowned.

"Again, what can I help you with?" Hannah said, knocking her fist on the desk.

Looking at Margaret, Hannah realized how many features they shared. Lips, chin, nose, almost identical eye color. Hannah stared for another moment, then jerked and looked away. It turned her stomach knowing that she would be a spitting image of the woman sitting across from her in twenty years.

"I don't know where to start."

"Well spit it out, because I have a meeting with a client in twenty minutes, so it's now or never." That was a lie.

Margaret paused for effect, then murmured, "I need your help."

Hannah snorted. "You need my help? With what?"

"Emily. She's gone."

"What do you mean she's gone?" Hannah said, leaning forward.

"We haven't seen or talked to her in almost two years."

"Two years? You have a missing person case, right? What do the local police or FBI say?"

"The FBI says they can't do anything because *technically* she's not missing." She paused for a second. "Because we know exactly where she is."

"Margaret, you're not making any sense. What do you mean exactly?"

For the first time since entering the office, Margaret turned away from Hannah. "It's an extremely convoluted situation, and even if I were composed, I wouldn't be able to give you all the details because I don't even know them, Steve does."

"How about you try?"

Margaret let out a deep sigh, then inhaled and let out

another. "First she dropped out of CSU. Then she moved to Utah and started going to these meetings, and then she joined this group, a cult or something, and then she just stopped talking to us."

"In Utah? I'm not going to be able to help. You need to hire someone local."

"We have, and we still haven't been able to talk to her," Margaret said, her voice growing louder with each word. "I'm just asking you to meet with Steve. He'll tell you everything."

"I don't see the purpose, because I honestly don't think I could help."

"Is this about money? Cause he is willing to pay a hefty reward to whoever can bring her home. I promise it'll be worth your while."

"No, it's not the money. I just ..."

"Then what is it, Hannah? Why can't you just meet with him?"

"I know you think the world revolves around you, and you don't have the slightest clue about my life, but I'm fucking busy with work. I've got more cases than I can handle right now, and I can't take on any more." That last part was another lie.

"I understand why you hate me. I also hate myself for what I did to you, but I can't fix any of that, no matter what I do, and I'm so sorry for that, Hannah." Margaret cleared her throat. "I wouldn't be here if I didn't think you couldn't help, so please meet with Steve. Just hear what he has to say. Nothing more."

"I wish I could help find her, but I just can't get involved right now."

Margaret's lips quivered as she began ruffling through her purse. For a moment, Hannah thought she was going to remove her checkbook, but she placed Steve's business card, face-up, in the middle of the desk. Margaret forced a smile, then got up and walked out of the office, not saying another word.

Four days later, Hannah was standing in the lobby outside Steve's office on the forty-ninth floor of the Cash Register building in downtown Denver. An exotic scent was in the air, like the air pumped into casinos. The floor seemed to sway, but she wasn't sure if it was real or in her imagination.

To her best recollection, she'd never been higher than twenty stories, so being almost five hundred feet off the ground put a pit in her stomach. She eased back into the leather couch and took the last remaining sips from her water bottle, then screwed the lid back on and carefully placed the empty bottle on the floor.

"He's wrapping up a call, and should be with you in a few minutes," said the receptionist. "Can I get you something to drink while you wait? Water? Coffee? A latte?"

"If it's not too much trouble, I'll take another water," Hannah said, pointing at the empty bottle.

"No problem at all."

The receptionist slid out from behind the desk and walked past Hannah and out of sight. She returned with a bottle of San Pellegrino. Hannah clinked the glass a few times with her fingernails, then opened it and took a sip.

On the wall hung black-and-white landscape photographs—all signed by Ansel Adams. Each photo was probably worth more than her car. She studied each picture for a few moments before moving on to the next one. When she finished, she peered back to the receptionist. The girl smiled briefly, then looked away.

Minutes passed, then the receptionist said, "He'll see you now."

Steve's office was larger than her entire apartment, yet oddly there was only a desk, a laptop, two chairs and about another dozen Ansel Adams photographs.

As she walked toward the desk, Steve got up and greeted her.

"Sorry for making you wait. Something urgent came up. I see Rachel already got you something to drink. Do you need anything else? We have a pantry full of snacks."

Hannah shook it off. "No, I'm good." She turned to one of the pictures. "Quite the Ansel Adams collection you have."

"Yes, growing up I wanted to be a photographer, and after discovering his work, my goal was to be the next Adams." He turned to a photograph of the Grand Canyon, admired it for a few moments, then turned back to Hannah. "I went to that exact location and took about a hundred pictures, and nothing came close to that one. I knew right then I wasn't meant to be a photographer, so I decided to go to law school and become a collector instead."

Immediately, Hannah regretted her comment. The last thing she wanted was a casual conversation with Steve. "It looks like a great collection and all, but can we skip to the part about why I'm here?"

"Yes, yes. Please take a seat," Steve said, gesturing to one of the chairs.

Sitting, Hannah peered beyond Steve to the skyline out the window. The view stretched hundreds of miles, from downtown Denver to the foothills, to the snow-covered peaks dotted along the Front Range.

"Quite the view huh?" Steve said, swiveling his chair about thirty degrees. "I've been in this office so long that sometimes I take it for granted."

"It beats my view of parking lots and I-25," she said sarcastically.

Steve smiled. "I really appreciate you meeting on such short notice."

Hannah nodded. "Margaret was somewhat vague about the situation, so I really don't have any details other than Emily is missing." Even though Hannah detested Margaret, and Steve to some degree, she had a weakness for missing person cases, especially ones involving women. In the end, she almost always said yes.

"Maggie, I think, she is having a very difficult—" He paused, searching for the perfect words. "She is distraught by Emily's disappearance, I mean rightfully so, but that makes it very challenging for her to talk about. I, on the other hand, am used to discussing difficult topics."

Hannah began second-guessing her decision to come here. For a moment, she thought about walking out and not saying a word, never speaking to him or Margaret again.

Steve tapped on the desk. "I get the feeling you don't want to be here, so let me lay everything out, give you all the details I have, and after I'm done, see if this is a case you might want to take on. Deal?"

She nodded. Hannah had also never trusted Steve—she always got ambulance chaser vibes from him, but with a nicer suit, office, and zip code.

"I've hired a half dozen PIs. A few ex-cops—one who specializes in missing persons, another was an ex-marine who served in the Gulf War, and the last one was an investigator who's an expert in surveillance—and I'm nowhere closer to Emily than a handful of pictures."

Steve spread five 6x9 color pictures on the table, fanning them out like a deck of cards. They were close-ups of Emily, probably captured by a very expensive telephoto lens. Hannah studied the pictures. The last time she'd seen

Emily was in a family Christmas card photo some years ago, and Hannah barely recognized her.

"These were taken last year, and until I saw them, I wasn't sure if she was alive or dead. And as pathetic as it sounds, these pictures have given me more hope than I've had since she disappeared."

"Where is she? Some sort of compound?"

He nodded. "At the Seven Day Saints property in Echo Canyon, Utah."

Hannah thought for a moment. The name sounded familiar, but she couldn't place it. "I don't think I've ever heard of it. Should I know about this place?"

"No, and that's by plan. They make a very concerted effort to keep a low profile."

"Who are they?"

"They refer to themselves as a fundamentalist group, but they are the definition of a cult, more akin to something like The Peoples Temple than any organized religion. They have small sects just north of the border in Alberta and one in Chihuahua, Mexico, but the majority of the members live in Echo Canyon, a small desert town a few miles north of the Utah-Arizona border."

"Are they a sect of the LDS?"

"Nope. The only common bond between the two is Utah; beyond that there's no connection." He took a sip of coffee. "It was started outside of Garden City, Kansas, in 1949 by a man named Noah Pratt. He lectured a combination of Christianity, Catholicism, science-fiction, new age beliefs, and some aspects of the Mayan calendar. It's like the guy went to the library and checked out a bunch of books on religion, mythology, and spirituality, selected the parts that he liked, then started preaching to whoever would listen."

"Sounds like how most cults start."

"Exactly, and I think he set out with the right intention, but it seems like something corrupted him along the way. Hell, the Peoples Temple and Jim Jones started off as a sanctuary for some, but we both know how that turned out."

When Hannah had woken up that morning, she hadn't thought she'd be getting a theology lesson, and she wasn't sure if she was prepared for one now. Never a religious person, she always steered clear when it came up in conversation.

"Well, it remained somewhat fringe for a few years, with only a few hundred members coming and going. Then in 1952, Noah was sentenced to seven years for aggravated assault. He nearly beat his wife to death." Steve shifted in his chair. "After an early release for good behavior, he gathered his wife, his first-born son Kenneth, and the few dozen remaining members, and they migrated west to Utah and founded Echo Canyon. The population steadily grew until the late 1970s, but after Noah died in 1990, Kenneth took over as leader, and the population grew exponentially to a few thousand. Pretty much what it is today."

"Any particular reason for the growth?" Hannah said.

"It seems like he became aggressive with their so-called missionary work. Going to colleges, homeless shelters, woman's shelters, AA meetings. He sought out vulnerable and impressionable people, and it worked." Steve paused for a moment. "Another reason is that before Noah died, he and only a select few others in the inner circle of Seven Day Saints could have plural marriages, but once Kenneth took over, he expanded that to every male in Echo Canyon. This has resulted in a baby boom over the last two decades."

"Fucking polygamy? What fucking century is it?"

"Yes." Steve nodded. "When Noah died, he had over

ten wives, some of them as young as teenagers, and days after the funeral, Kenneth took them all as his own wives."

"Lovely. Sounds like they had a very strong father-son relationship."

"And that isn't even all of his wives. I've read some estimates that Kenneth has somewhere between twenty and thirty, and probably double or triple that many kids, but nobody outside of Echo Canyon really knows."

"I might be mistaken, but I thought polygamy was illegal in the US, even in Utah," Hannah said.

"Polygamy is just touching the surface. There are reports of rape, assaults, child abuse, forced marriage. Some of the girls who are forced into marriage are as young as thirteen."

Hannah thought over that, trying to comprehend everything that Steve was telling her.

"You said a few thousand people, right? A town that big must have a police department, some sort of local law enforcement."

Steve smiled. "Oh, there is, but every member of the police force, from the chief of police down to the deputies, is a member of Seven Day Saints."

"That seems like a problem," Hannah said.

"Exactly. That is why we can't get close to Emily." Steve tapped his knuckles on the desk.

Hannah leaned forward to look at the pictures of Emily again. "How did she end up here?"

"She wanted to take a year off from school. I was against it, but every time we talked, I could hear the anxiety in her voice. She didn't like some of her professors, and she started falling behind in her courses, and at the same time she was dealing with a very messy break-up, and was—I guess just lost, unsure what to do with her life. Looking back now, I feel so careless that I missed the obvious signs and didn't realize how severe her depression was. All I cared about was her getting into law school, so I was against the break, but Emily is stubborn like me, so I knew she would do it with or without my approval. So, I caved, and told her she could drop out for a year."

The building swayed again, and Hannah took a deep breath. She started picking at the cuticle on her thumb, trying to subdue her anxiety.

Steve forced a smile that quickly faded. "She always wanted to live in the Southwest, so she packed up and moved to Utah. After bouncing around a couple places, she ended up in Springdale, outside of Zion. She worked at this tour group doing customer service, and she loved it. I don't remember hearing her sounding so happy. It really made me think college might not be right for her after all."

Maybe it was because he was a lawyer, but his speech was mechanical, lacking empathy. That troubled Hannah.

"Within weeks, she became friends with some of her coworkers, and one of them was a member of Seven Day Saints. Emily went to a few retreats, and then she started visiting Echo Canyon. At the beginning, she kept telling me what an amazing place it was. That Kenneth changed her entire outlook on life. Every conversation I had with her was, 'These people are like no one I've ever met. They're all happy, and all they talk about is love. There is no hate. Just love. The more she got involved with them, the less she called. From twice a week, to weekly, to once or twice a month. The last few calls, there was something in her voice that gave me a bad feeling. So, I start investigating them and realized they are a cult. I called and told her she had to come home immediately." Steve let out a long sigh. "That was the last time I talked to her."

"When was that?" Hannah said.

"Nearly two years ago."

"Did you ever go out there and look for her?"

"Yeah, twice. The first time I went directly to the police department and explained everything. The following day they called me back and told me they'd spoken to her, and she was safe. She was an adult and she was there of her own will, so there was nothing they could do to help."

"That was their nice way of telling you to fuck off."

"Yeah. The second time I went, I booked a week at the only motel, with the hope of seeing her out and about. I ate every meal at the local restaurants, hung around town, went to the parks, and attempted to talk to anyone I came in contact with. Half the people didn't respond, like they were mute. The other half pretty much shrugged and said they didn't know her, had never seen her; some said they thought she skipped town. I've been a lawyer for a very long time, so I have a pretty good bullshit detector, and I knew almost everyone was lying.

"Well, at the end of my week, I decided to extend my stay, and I went to book a few more nights, and they said they were completely booked. There wasn't another person at the motel or another car in the parking lot. That's when I knew I wasn't going to be able to find her, and I was going to have to hire a professional."

"Yeah, they're not going to let you get anywhere close to her," Hannah said.

Steve nodded slowly, his eyes on one of the Ansel Adams photographs.

Hannah tried to remember Emily's birthday. "Is she twenty-one? Twenty-two?"

"Twenty-one next month."

"Have you ever considered she doesn't want to talk to you anymore? Maybe she finds some sort of fulfillment within the group, and that's why when you were there, she hid from you."

Steve tapped his knuckles on the desk again, trying to mask his frustration. "Yes, I've considered that, and it could be a possibility, and if she wants to stay there, there isn't much that can be done. I'll have to live with that." He was direct, at least. "But I want confirmation from her that she is okay, and she is there of her own volition. From her mouth to my ears."

"And you think I can get that confirmation?" Hannah said, pointing at her chest.

"Yes, I do."

"I mean, I think I'm a very talented investigator, but from the sounds of it, you've already hired some accomplished PIs and all they could get are these pictures. What makes you believe I can succeed where they all failed?"

"She knows you," he said.

Hannah cracked a smile. "You really think she'll recognize me? It's been damn near a decade since I've seen her. She wasn't even in high school."

"I know for a fact she will. She adored you. She talked about you all the time."

That was perplexing. Aside from Thanksgiving and their time playing Uno, Hannah had only seen Emily a handful of times, and never once after that trip. Their time together had been pleasant, but Hannah had never had a desire to forge a stepsister relationship.

Steve turned back to the skyline. "I wish your mother and I would've had you around more often."

"Please don't call her that," Hannah said, her voice low.

"Sorry, I just think if Margaret and I would've done a lot of things differently, we wouldn't be in this situation," Steve said, staring in the void. "All I'm asking is for three days. If after that you feel like you can't help bring Emily home, I'll accept your decision and be forever in your gratitude."

"I'm not in the practice of taking jobs from clients if I don't think I can help them."

"Please, I'm begging you," he said, fighting back tears. "I just need her home."

The look of despair in his eyes was something Hannah had seen numerous times when talking to the parents of a missing child. It never got easier, never. She was certain the case was futile, that the odds of locating and then speaking to Emily were very slim, but she didn't have the strength to decline.

Hannah let out a long sigh. "Three days?"

"Yes. I want you to meet with Roger. He was the one who took these pictures, and he pretty much uncovered more information than everyone else combined. If, after talking to him, you think it is hopeless, then I'll accept that and will continue my search for someone who can find her."

"And where is he?"

"Cortez. In southern Colorado."

"Cortez? That's like eight hours away. Can't I just call the guy?"

"No. You're not just going to Cortez. He's going to take you to Echo Canyon. I want you to see it with your own eyes and get a sense of where Emily is. The town, the compound, the people, everything."

"And you're going to pay me my normal rate to take a three-day road trip across the Southwest?"

"I'll pay that plus a 20 percent bonus."

Hannah bit her bottom lip and turned away. It took her a few seconds to answer, but she'd already decided. "Okay, I'll meet him."

THREE

Thick, gray clouds hung in the Montezuma Valley as Hannah drove past the "Welcome to Cortez" sign. The town sat less than ten miles from Mesa Verde National Park, home to some of the largest cliff dwellings in the world, dating back thousands of years. As she drove past the entrance to the park, a memory that she hadn't thought about in a very long time surfaced.

Before Casey's murder, Hannah was enrolled in Colorado Adventures, a summer youth program that offered backpacking expeditions to state and national parks, including Mesa Verde. But after Casey died, she withdrew from the program. Hannah never made it to Mesa Verde or Cortez or anywhere else she'd dreamed of visiting as a kid.

Roger lived on the outskirts of Cortez, in the Verde Village, a mobile home community where most of the homes were in disrepair, some likely close to being condemned. Siding missing, pieces of plywood in place of windows, piles of trash littered on porches in the place of patio furniture. Kids played in the road, throwing rocks with little regard to collateral damage to cars, houses, and people, seemingly oblivious of her vehicle.

She parked in a dirt driveway in front of Roger's double wide, a hidden gem in the community, and took the final sips of her gas station coffee. Struggling to keep her eyes open, Hannah considered checking into her room and taking a quick nap, but she feared if she did, she might not wake up until morning.

As she stepped onto the porch, a dog barked somewhere to the south, answered by another in the distance. The barking grew louder, rising to a sudden howl, and then silence fell.

Hannah was about to press the doorbell when a rough voice said, "Come in, the door is unlocked."

When Hannah stepped in, the man was standing in the middle of the kitchen like he'd been in that exact position for hours, waiting for her. His head was within inches of the ceiling, and he must've weighed close to three hundred pounds. He looked more like an offensive lineman than a private detective. His thick, black hair hung over his shoulders, and he wore a black cowboy hat with tribal beaded bands containing turquoise, orange, yellow, and red. A large feather flared out from the band.

Hannah thought he resembled William Sampson from *One Flew Over the Cuckoo's Nest*, and for some reason that comparison made her feel uncomfortable.

"Hannah, Hannah Jacobs," he said, staring down at her.

"Yes, and I assume you're Roger Walker," she said, offering her hand.

His hand was massive, and his fingers nearly crushed hers—likely unaware of his own strength.

"Steve tells me you want to see Echo Canyon."

When he spoke, the left side of his face did not move—complete paralysis. She suspected a stroke, or perhaps a neurological disorder.

"I personally wanted this to be a phone call, but he insisted I come, so here I am." Hannah shrugged. "According to him, you seem to have the most knowledge of the case. Give me the odds of finding Emily and bringing her home."

He thought for a moment. "Slim. I'm not certain if she wants to leave."

"Well, that's going to make it hard to get her out then."

He tried to smile. "So, you are a private investigator?"

"Yes. Pretty much the only job I've ever had."

"How did Steve find you?"

Hannah stared. "Does it matter?"

"Yes, it does. This isn't some summer camp that you can stroll in and out of. These are some very dangerous people."

"Well, if you need to know, Steve is married to the woman you could technically call my biological mother," she said, cringing as she uttered the word.

"So, your stepdad then?"

Steve must've told Roger who she was. So, why was he asking these questions?

"I don't use that term, but I guess you can call him that." Hannah leaned back into the kitchen counter. "And just so you know, I'm a very accomplished PI. I've done a lot more than workers' comp and infidelity cases, and I've actually solved a few missing persons cases, believe it or not. Next time I'll bring my resume."

He studied Hannah for a while, twisting a toothpick between his lips like he was pondering a complex mathematical formula.

"If I were you, I'd be very cautious of what Steve told

you about Echo Canyon. He only has one interest in mind, and that is to bring home Emily, and that supersedes the safety of everyone involved."

Hannah smiled. "Thanks for the warning, but you don't have to worry about me. I'll be fine."

Roger nodded. "What do you know about Kenneth Pratt and Seven Day Saints?"

It'd been one week since she'd met with Steve, and she'd intended to do thorough research, but between her caseload and her growing alcoholism, she'd only found a few spare hours.

Kenneth Pratt, age forty-six, had been born in Garden City. No criminal record, no speeding ticket, not even as much as a parking ticket. He married Peggy Reed in 1978, when they were both twenty-three, and there was no record of divorce. The only jobs he'd worked had been various positions at Seven Day Saints: secretary, treasurer, counselor, inner circle member, and finally leader. He'd never reported making more than $40,000 a year and had never owed taxes.

As for information on Seven Day Saints, that was tougher to uncover, and what she did find was disturbing. Their motto was "Love Thy Brother and Sister," and it was plastered throughout Echo Canyon—in houses, in the churches, in the school, in stores, and even on mailboxes. Their teachings stated that anyone who wasn't a member of Seven Day Saints was indeed not a brother or sister and in fact was the devil in disguise.

Seven Day Saints believed marriage of the same sex and outside of one race was a sin. They prohibited drinking, smoking, profanity, masturbation, and sex outside of wedlock. Even sex between a husband and wife was only allowed when the woman was ovulating. TV was forbidden, and all literature had to be approved by Seven Day Saints.

Then there was the real wild shit, like their insistence that the earth was only five hundred years old, and dinosaurs never existed, and strangely that the Apollo missions were faked and man had never been to space.

"I wouldn't be surprised if these fucks believe the moon was made out of cheese," Hannah said.

"Neither would I," Roger said.

Hannah continued. They were seemingly left to their own accord until an FBI raid in 1992. After the operation was complete, no evidence of any illegal activity was found, and no members of Seven Day Saints were charged. The raid was an embarrassment to the FBI, and that was the last documented time any government agency had stepped foot on the property.

Roger stared for a moment when she finished. "That's a good start, I'll fill you in on the rest during the drive."

"Like, right now?" Hannah said.

"Yes, now."

"I'm pretty beat. I was hoping to go to my room tonight. I just want a shower, a beer, a burger, and bed. Can we leave first thing in the morning?"

Roger shook his head slowly. "Like I said, these people are very dangerous, and I will not go there during daylight hours."

"That's the second time you've used the word 'dangerous.' Just for reference, how dangerous are we talking? On a scale of one to ten, with one being they like to litter and ten they're as deadly as Hannibal Lecter."

Roger walked over to a bookshelf, each step heavy, creating a minor tremor. He picked up a wooden frame, then handed it to Hannah. Inside was a picture of Roger kneeling next to a dog, probably a golden retriever. At the bottom of the frame, engraved into the wood, was the name "Dakota."

"They killed her."

Hannah looked at him. "Are you being serious?"

"I wouldn't make a joke about my Dakota."

"How?"

"They poisoned her," he said in a rough voice.

"How the fuck did they do that?

Roger extended his hand, and Hannah returned the frame. He kissed the picture. Then he placed it back in the exact position on the shelf.

"I let her out one morning last summer while I was reading the paper, drinking my coffee. Normally she'd do her business and come back in. Well, after about ten minutes, I glance out the window and see she'd fallen over. I ran out, and when I get to her, she was convulsing. I picked her up and placed her in my truck, then sped to the vet. By the time I got there, she wasn't breathing, and there wasn't anything they could do to save her. Dead within the hour."

"I'm so sorry," Hannah said, barely able to string the words together.

"The vet thought it was probably something with her heart. When I got home, I grabbed a shovel and went into the backyard to find a proper burial location, and as I was surveying the land, I saw something in the grass. It was a piece of cheese wrapped around a pill. I did a perimeter search and found four more. I have a friend at the Montezuma Forensic Lab, and he tested them, and they all came back positive for cyanide."

"And you think it was someone at Seven Day Saints?" Hannah said.

"I don't think, I know it was," Roger said. "I spent two full days searching every lot in this community, and I didn't find another pill. Not a single fucking one. The only ones were on my property. It had to be them. I was doing surveillance on them weeks earlier, and I had an uneasy feeling I'd been made."

"That is some evil shit. I've never heard of anything like that before."

Roger stared straight ahead, seemingly fighting back tears. "If you can't tell, I prefer the company of animals more than people, so I was closer to Dakota than anyone else I know. I don't think I've ever been so distraught over someone dying." He let out a deep sigh. "It took every ounce of strength not to drive to that compound with guns blazing, but I knew that would result in innocent casualties. Mark my word, though, I will get my revenge one day. I can promise you that."

"I still can't wrap my head around how anyone could do that to a dog,"

"I told you they were very dangerous," Roger said. He looked back into the living room and pointed to a brindle whippet curled up on a rug. "That's Kona, and I will not put her life in jeopardy. That's why we leave now. We'll be far away from Echo Canyon before sunrise."

"She's beautiful," Hannah said.

Roger smiled. "You wouldn't know it by looking at her, but that breed is one of the fastest dogs on the planet, and one of the best small game hunters you'll find. She can catch a rabbit like nobody's business."

"I guess you don't have to worry about any critters ransacking your garden then."

Roger ignored her poor attempt at humor. "Do you need to use the bathroom before we leave? I don't want to make any unplanned stops."

Hannah shook her head.

"Okay. I've got a thermos full of coffee, and everything else we'll need is in my truck." He glanced at his watch. "As long as there are no construction delays, we should be there sometime around midnight."

"Five hours?" she said, letting out a heavy sigh.

"You can sleep if you need to. I've driven this route so many times I can almost do it with my eyes closed."

As they drove past Four Corners Monument, the sun disappeared across the high desert. The radio began losing reception, the talk station going from sporadic static to intermittent static to complete static over the course of a few miles. Roger reached down and turned it off.

"And if you're wondering what's wrong with my face, I had Bell's Palsy a few years ago," he said, as if continuing a conversation, though they'd been driving in silence. "Most people fully recover. I unfortunately did not." He looked straight ahead, never taking his eyes off the road. "Everyone thinks it's a stroke."

"Yeah, that is what I thought."

"That's why I just come out and tell people. It erases the mystery of what happened."

The cab fell silent again. After they'd passed about a dozen road signs, Hannah finally said, "You never told me your insights about Kenneth Pratt."

"Your typical cult leader. Power hungry, manipulative, smart. He claims that his bloodline can be traced back to Benjamin Franklin, but I can't find any records to prove it. No one knows how many children he has, but I wouldn't be surprised if it was over fifty."

Roger blew his nose into a handkerchief, then stuffed it back into his front pocket. "Are you familiar with Jim Jones?"

"Yeah. Peoples Temple, Kool-Aid laced with cyanide. Mass suicide down in South America."

"Yep, but the mass suicide notion is a misconception. Most of those people were forced to drink the Kool-Aid knock-off Flavor-Aid. There's a tape that was released—some people referred to it as the death tape. Well, it's a recording with Jim Jones rambling on, convincing people to drink the punch, and in the background, you can hear screaming, babies crying, people pleading that they don't want to die." Roger took a long beat. "I hope I'm wrong, but I wouldn't be surprised if that happens to the people of Echo Canyon one day."

"I really hope you're wrong too."

Out of the corner of her eye, Hannah saw something on the shoulder. At first, she couldn't tell if it was a person or an animal, then at about three hundred feet, she made out the silhouette of a man.

Roger slowed, turned on the hazards, and asked Hannah to roll down the window. He leaned over the center console. "Hey buddy, are you doing okay?"

The man looked at Hannah, then acknowledged Roger before turning back to her. His head barely moved, and his lips remained tight.

Roger asked the man again, almost yelling, but he remained still. Then Roger spoke in a language she'd never heard before. Maybe Navajo or Ute. The man surveyed the truck, then replied in the same language. The exchange went back and forth five or six times. Roger raised his hand and waved, and the man nodded and continued along the road.

"He said he got in an argument with his wife and was just letting off some steam, so it wouldn't escalate," Roger said. "His house is about a mile up over that hill, and he didn't need a ride. Then he thanked us and wished us good luck on our journey."

"You told him what we were doing?"

"No, I think it was just intuition."

Hannah was about to respond, but she just gave a silent nod instead.

The land was endless. She searched for anything that resembled a structure, but after about a minute, she gave up and returned her gaze to the road and its string of highway lines.

"Is that common out here?" she asked.

"Unfortunately, yes. It is a very poor region. A lot of people don't have cars, and if they do, they can't afford gas. Some don't have indoor plumbing, so they bathe and do laundry in lakes, and some can't afford electricity, so they live by candlelight. You'll see more stray dogs than deer, because people can't afford neutering." Roger cleared his throat. "And to top all that off, the rate of alcoholism and addiction is some of the highest in the country. I myself have had two uncles and three cousins who died of either cirrhosis or liver failure. If you're Native American, you most likely know someone who has died from addiction.

"Besides my nana, who lived well into her eighties, I'm the oldest out of anyone in my immediate family. Both my parents died in their forties, and I probably would've been dead by now if I had ever picked up a bottle, but luckily, I had enough sense to never start."

"I had no idea," Hannah said.

"Most people don't, and most of the ones that do don't care."

Unsure what to say, Hannah watched as the minutes ticked away on the digital clock. She was exhausted, and the caffeine was useless.

Shortly after they passed through Kayenta, Hannah decided she could no longer keep her eyes open. She balled her coat up in a weak attempt at a pillow, placed it against the window, and brought her knees to her chest.

"I've been up since five, so I'm going to close my eyes for a bit if that's fine by you."

Roger nodded as the engine roared.

When Hannah awoke, the truck was parked on the shoulder, with the engine idling and the headlights on. Roger was nowhere in sight. After searching for a few moments, she felt a slight panic set in.

As she was about to step out, Roger stood up in front of the truck, holding up the license plates.

Climbing back into the cab, he slipped the plates under the bucket seat, then handed Hannah a screwdriver. "Will you put this back in the glovebox?"

Hannah was about to ask why he'd removed the plates, but she realized she already knew the answer. Better safe than sorry.

Instead, she said, "Where are we?"

"About twenty minutes from the turnoff to Echo Canyon," he said, shifting gears. "We're getting real close."

Shortly after passing mile marker 119, Roger slowed the truck and turned on the blinker. Even though there probably wasn't another vehicle for miles, Hannah appreciated the courtesy.

He pulled onto the dirt road, drove over the cattle guard, turned on the brights, and stopped. Gripping the steering wheel, he stared straight ahead. The headlights vanished after about forty feet, leaving nothing but a black canvas.

"Buckle up. This next part gets a little bumpy," Roger said.

"I'm already buckled."

"Well, hold on to something then."

For the next thirty-five minutes, they traversed some of the roughest road Hannah had ever been on. She bounced around like a rag doll, and twice almost hit her head on the roof.

Roger parked next to a juniper tree and turned off the lights and the engine.

"What are we doing?" Hannah said.

"It's about a mile up," he said, pointing into the night.

"And we're not going to drive?"

"No, ma'am. I'm not risking them seeing my headlights shine down onto the canyon walls. Anyways, if we cut straight up the ridge, we'll get a better view."

"It would've been nice to know that some hiking was involved."

"It's not that bad, I promise," Roger said, grabbing a backpack off the floorboard. "And I have everything we'll need. Gloves, a blanket, flashlights, and night-vision binoculars."

Roger handed her a pair of gloves. Hannah slipped her hand into the left one. There was almost enough room for both of her hands. "A little big, don't you think?"

"They will do the job," he said, securing his backpack. "Before we go, there are a couple strict rules I need you to follow."

"I'm listening."

"One. Watch your step when we get to the cliff edge. It's a few hundred feet straight down to the canyon floor."

Heights were something Hannah avoided at all costs, and her pulse began to race knowing that when they arrived at the cliff, she'd feel the urge to step over. After a deep breath, she told herself it was all in her head.

"Two. When I tell you to turn off the flashlight, turn it off, and keep it off. If they see any light or any unknown activity, they'll send out a party to investigate. Three.

When I say it's time to leave, we leave. If you follow those three simple rules, we should have a lovely evening. Do you have any questions?"

"Nope, I think I can handle all that."

"Good, follow me," Roger said, turning on the flashlight.

They trudged up the ridge, breaking trail with each step. The terrain was tough going, and Hannah had to stop every few hundred feet to catch her breath, placing her hands on her knees. Sweat dripped down her forehead and into her eyes as her chest thundered. Nothing like a hike up an unmarked trail to bring on the sensation of a heart attack.

Each time she stopped, she glanced up at Roger, and even though he was at least twice her age, he didn't show any signs that he was winded. Almost like he was taking a casual morning stroll around a city lake.

It took some forty minutes to reach the rim of the canyon. Roger knelt and turned back to Hannah.

"Okay, it's time to turn off the flashlights. When we do, it'll be very dark, so we'll just stay here for a minute or two and let our eyes adjust," he said under his breath.

They both turned off their flashlights, and within moments there was a small glow over the ridge visible to the west.

"I take it that's Echo Canyon," Hannah said.

"Yes. Are you ready?"

At first Hannah nodded. Then she realized he probably couldn't see her, so she murmured, "Yeah, let's go."

Roger spread a blanket over the gravel and handed Hannah a pair of night-vision binoculars. She took them, then made her way carefully to the cliff.

"Easy over there, some of the rock is very loose," Roger whispered.

What lay below gave her a sinister feeling. Silent. Cold. Terrifying. She'd felt it a handful of times before, the last being when she stood face-to-face with Terry Stone. The longer she stood there, the more uneasy she felt.

Hannah stepped back until she was on the blanket, then dropped to her stomach, propped her elbows on the ground, and began surveying the land through the binoculars. The plastic was cold against her face.

"There is the headquarters for Seven Day Saints," Roger said. The binoculars in his hands resembled a kid's toy.

A two-story building, roughly the size of a high school gymnasium, sat directly in front of them near the base of the valley walls. About a dozen mobile homes surrounded the main building in a half circle, with a barn set a few hundred feet farther back. A dirt parking lot lay in the front of the main building, with three cars and two passenger vans. The light from the buildings shone onto the canyon walls until it faded into darkness.

A faint, constant hum filled the air, probably the electricity emitting from the compound.

"The main building is where Kenneth and I think a few of the inner circle members of Seven Day Saints live. The mobile homes house women and children. I suspect they're Kenneth's wives and kids."

"Have you seen inside the main building? Pictures? Blueprints?"

"Nah, I pulled some old building plans, but from the looks of it, it's probably three times the size now. Who knows how much work has been done over the years? And to no surprise, they're not pulling permits for new construction."

As Hannah continued surveying the compound, a gust swept over the ridge and blew gravel into their faces. The binoculars protected Hannah's eyes, but tiny dirt particles flew into her mouth. She turned and spat twice, but some pieces remained, grinding against her teeth every time she moved her jaw.

"And this is where you took the pictures of Emily?"

"Yes. I got positive ID on her twice. The first time she circled the grounds a few times with an unidentified male. The second time was on that bench, about a hundred feet north of the barn. She sat there alone for nearly twenty minutes."

"What was she doing?

"Nothing. She didn't have a book or newspaper or anything. She just sat there and stared right back toward me."

"Kind of like she was waiting for you to take her picture."

"It did feel like that."

"And there was no way she could know you were sitting here?"

"At that time, I was certain I was undetected, but looking back, I don't know."

"Do you think she's living in one of those buildings?" Hannah whispered, like someone was eavesdropping.

"That I don't know for certain, but I've never seen her outside the compound, nor have any of the other investigators." He paused. "I told Steve this and he didn't want to hear it, but most of the women that live on the compound appear to be Kenneth's wives, so I assume she might be one as well."

For the next few minutes, Hannah scanned the compound, searching for any movement, but there was no one.

"How far is the main building from here?"

"Rough calculations, I'd say it's probably around fourteen hundred meters."

Hannah lowered the binoculars. "I went to a public school in the US, so you're going to have to help a girl out with the metric conversion."

"Almost a mile. There's sixteen hundred meters in a mile."

"Thanks, that's exactly what I needed to hear."

"Now if you go south from the parking lot, you'll run right into the guard station. It's about eight hundred meters." He paused for a second. "Or half a mile. And that's the only road into the compound."

"One road in, and one road out," Hannah said, mostly to herself.

"And the only way to get to the road is if you drive through town, which is about seven miles away, so if anyone attempted to raid them, someone in town could easily alert people in the compound and they'd at least have a five, maybe ten-minute warning."

"Smart. A nice buffer to hide or dispose of any illegal activity in case anyone is going to have a surprise visit. Do you know if the guards are armed?"

"I haven't seen them with any firearms, but I've heard there's a stockpile of weapons in the main building that would make most terrorist groups jealous."

Hannah studied the guard station. Nothing moved. If she didn't know better, she could've mistaken the figures for elaborate decoys, setup as a trap. After some time, one of the guards walked out of the building, looked up, then returned.

The moon hung directly overhead, casting a spotlight down on them. And even though she was certain they were invisible, the radiant night sky did little to calm her nerves.

"We're safe up here, right?" she said.

"This is probably the safest location to view the compound and town."

"That response doesn't give me confidence."

"We'll only be 100 percent safe when we're back in my truck and on our way back to Colorado."

"How close have you ever gotten?"

"You're looking at it, sweetheart. I don't think a three-hundred-pound Indian with a paralyzed face would be able to stroll around town and stay under the radar."

"Yeah, I guess you'd probably stick out like a sore thumb."

"A sore thumb? More like a damn alien. That is the whitest damn town I've ever seen."

They began to laugh, but then stopped abruptly as Hannah heard rustling in the bush about a hundred feet behind them.

"It's probably just a rabbit," Roger whispered.

Hannah watched warily, fear overcoming her. Maybe it was a rabbit, maybe it wasn't. Maybe someone from Seven Day Saints had followed them up here. After twenty seconds, the rustling stopped. She watched for another twenty seconds, then slowly turned back.

"What's that opening behind the barn?"

"That is Echo Canyon. If you follow the route from there, it's about twenty miles to Highway 99, give or take a few."

"Can you get to the compound through the canyon from the highway?"

"Technically yes, but the terrain is extremely treacherous. The rock walls rise a few hundred feet in some spots, and flash floods occur on seemingly cloudless days, and in the summer, temps on the canyon floor can reach up to 130 degrees. It's also a labyrinth of canyons and gullies, and trails that only experienced backcountry hikers should navigate. If you take a wrong turn, you could hike twenty or thirty miles off course and run into a dead end. Two hikers died of exposure a couple winters ago about five miles directly north of here. They got lost, dehydrated, disoriented, ended up going in circles until they died. And that's not to mention the rattlesnakes, scorpions, and about a dozen other things that would love to kill you."

"What about a four-wheeler? Or an ATV?"

"No can do. Some of the boulders are bigger than a Volkswagen Beetle, so I doubt many vehicles could maneuver them."

"So, they have the front on complete lockdown, and they're protected in the back by an impassable canyon. Sounds like a pretty good place to start a cult."

"Yeah, it's no accident they chose this location. This might be one of the most remote towns in all of the Lower 48. The canyon walls act as a natural barrier to the north and east, to the west is almost a hundred miles of barren desert until I-15, and the only thing to the south is the Grand Canyon."

"What about the road that goes through Echo Canyon?"

"289? That's pretty much been obsolete since Highway 99 was completed sometime in the late '70s. It made it a straight shot from Page to St. George. I think unless you're hiking Wolf Buttes or doing some off-grid camping, or you're a member of Seven Day Saints, there isn't really a reason to take 289."

A sting coursed through her entire body, then lingered in her shoulder blades. She reached back and massaged them to ease the sensation. It didn't help.

"The town is a lot bigger than I thought," Hannah said, looking to Echo Canyon.

"Let's see, there are a few hundred houses, a school that serves K-12, two gas stations, a grocery store, a motel, a few restaurants. Pretty much everything you need to operate a small town. And Kenneth and Seven Day Saints own every building within the city limits."

"Every single building, huh?"

"Yes. He dictates where people live, where they work, how they spend their money. Hell, he even tells them how to vote. This county has some of the most unanimous elections in the country. Kenneth personally selects who runs for elected positions, and seemingly every resident of Echo Canyon votes for his candidates. The mayor, the sheriff—everyone answers to Kenneth. They probably don't jump unless he says so."

"And officials in Salt Lake City are okay with this?"

Roger chuckled. "His second cousin is a state senator, and he was one of the biggest donors for the governor's reelection. They're buddies. In fact, Kenneth went to the governor's daughter's wedding two summers ago."

"So, he has a free pass from local and state law enforcement to do whatever the fuck he wants?"

"Pretty much."

Hannah shook her head in disgust. "I can't believe a place like this exists."

"Better believe it, because it's real."

"And I bet since Kenneth has complete control over the town, he probably considers himself as some kind of God."

"No, it's much worse than that."

"How so?"

"The people of Echo Canyon believe he is one."

For the next five minutes or so, they watched the compound in complete silence. There was no activity. Finally, Hannah said, "If this is as close as you've gotten, how did they know you were surveilling them?"

"I was out here one morning, and I think there might've

been a glare from my binoculars. Well, someone in the guard station looked in my direction and pointed. I got a little spooked and went back to my room in Red Mesa. The next morning, I came back and there were footprints and tire tracks everywhere. I got the hell out of here and drove home, but I bet they were waiting for me down the road and got my license plate."

Roger gave a quick glance over his shoulder. "Come on, we need to go. It's only about an hour until sunrise."

Hannah handed him the binoculars, then picked up a rock the size of her hand and tossed it over the cliff. Even though she knew there wouldn't be a sound when it landed, she still turned her ear, waiting for it to crash to the canyon floor. Nothing.

"I've got a very bad feeling about this place," Hannah said.

"I always do when I'm out here. It usually doesn't subside until I cross the state line."

As Hannah stood, a slight drizzle began to fall. Her breath was a thick, white cloud. "Besides Steve, have you talked to anyone who's been to Echo Canyon?"

"I'm friendly with a reporter at the *Salt Lake Times*. He spent some time down there, working on an investigative piece about Kenneth and Seven Day Saints. Guess what happened?" Roger said.

"It never got published."

He nodded. "Three days before it was supposed to go to print, his editor told him that for legal reasons, they couldn't run anything about Kenneth or Seven Day Saints. He suspects the decision came from the owner."

"So, Kenneth controls the Utah media as well?"

Roger nodded. "After it got axed, he gave me some details of the story, and one of the people he interviewed was a girl named Marie. She grew up in Echo Canyon and was a member of Seven Day, along with her parents and brother, but she escaped about five years ago. Well, I asked if he'd get me in contact with her. She said yes, but would only talk on the phone, and each time it would cost $100."

"Did she actually talk to you?"

"Yeah, I called her four times. Most of what I know about Echo Canyon came from her. Her details are pristine. I told her she needs to write a book."

Hannah grabbed Roger's forearm, trying to stop him, but it was to no avail. Like a mouse fighting a gorilla. "Are you still in communication with her?"

"Unfortunately, no. I foolishly told her about Dakota, and I think that scared her away. It's been months since we've talked. And to answer your next question, the number is disconnected."

"Fuck, what about your reporter friend?"

"No. According to him, I talked to her more recently."

"So, there's no way I could talk to this girl?" Hannah said with a heavy sigh.

"Well, the last time we spoke, she was working in Las Vegas as an escort under the name of Roxy. That and a picture."

"So, I guess I'll just walk up and down the Strip, holding up the picture and yelling her name at the top of my lungs." Hannah kicked a rock, and in seconds it was out of sight. "There have to be thousands of escorts in Vegas. I could probably spend a year looking and never find her."

"If you really think talking to her will help with your investigation, that's what you'll have to do."

FOUR

As Hannah exited Circus Circus, a voice hissed at her from the shadows. "Nice tits."

She glanced at the disheveled man, who was sitting in his own filth, then continued walking without acknowledging him. She'd lost count of how many catcalls she'd endured during her time on Las Vegas Boulevard. At least two dozen, maybe many more.

"Marie, where the hell are you?" Hannah said to herself, staring up at the countless hotel rooms.

Casino after casino after casino—Luxor, The Venetian, Harrah's, The Mirage, Treasure Island, The Stardust. A concrete jungle illuminated by hundreds of flashing billboards and thousands of nameless faces.

Hannah talked to nearly every working girl she came across, showing them the picture of Marie that Roger had given her. "Do you know this girl?"

Almost every response was either "Sorry, I've never seen her" or "Fuck off, bitch."

Twice, she thought she had found Marie, once at a bar in Bally's and once at a craps table in Treasure Island, but both times, when Hannah got close, the woman was at least a decade older. The endless clamor of bells and chimes was making her delirious, causing her mind to play tricks on her.

As she traveled the Strip, she collected every escort magazine and card that a slapper flicked in her direction, men wearing fluorescent green and orange shirts with bold print: things like "Girls to Your Room in 20 Minutes" followed by a telephone number.

In a little over thirty hours, she had scoured what felt like every casino floor, every bar, and every nook and cranny of the Strip, probably covering at least ten miles. She only stopped searching three times—twice for an hour-long nap and once to eat a $1 foot-long hot dog that she had to choke down.

Her hair was greasy, her legs felt like Jello, and she had a bunch of blisters on the bottom of her feet. Her body was pungent, even to her, and at that moment, she was strongly considering forfeiting the search and going straight back to the room for an hour-long shower followed by enough meals for a family of four from room service, then a day-long slumber.

When she walked past the Bellagio, she stopped at the lake, leaned on the railing, and stared down into the water, letting her mind shut off for a moment. The exhaustion was becoming overwhelming, and she was unsure how much longer she could keep searching.

A few hours later, Hannah returned to her room, kicked off her shoes, and dumped the cards from her backpack onto the floor like a kid pouring out their bag of candy on Halloween. Hundreds of escort cards and at least a dozen magazines containing another few hundred escorts. It was going to be a very long night.

Hannah sorted the stack like a deck of cards, and by the time she was done, there were two piles, each at least three inches high. Each card fundamentally featured the same design, like they all came from the same printing press. A picture of a scantily clad woman with their name, their number, and a catchphrase like "Eager to Please," "For the Ultimate Evening," "Two for the Price of One." If someone had a fetish, their any desire could easily be fulfilled.

Hannah took a long pull from a bottle of whiskey, leaned against the bed, then grabbed the trash can and placed it between her legs. She picked up a stack and, using her index and middle fingers, began pushing each top card off, letting them tumble into the trash.

Minutes into the second stack, she stopped just as her fingers were about to dispose of another card.

Reaching back, Hannah grabbed the picture of Marie and held it side by side with the card. Printed across the girl's breasts was the name "Roxy," along with a number and the phrase "Good girl looking for a bad time." Beneath the mountain of makeup and difference in hair length and color, the faces were almost identical.

"Holy shit, this is her!" she yelled, dropping the rest of the cards to the floor.

Hannah stared at the card for a long time, occasionally flicking a corner with her finger. Maybe Lady Luck was on her side. For a moment, she considered going to the casino to place a bet on red, but she decided against it. Better not press her luck.

After another pull from the bottle, she slipped on her shoes and started to the elevator. About halfway down the hall, she jerked to a stop and returned to the room to grab a bottle of water.

If an elevator ride was more than a couple of stories, she never entered without something to drink. The thought of being trapped inside terrified her, but the idea of being stuck without a drink triggered a nightmare-inducing panic attack. She knew the odds were near zero, but that didn't ease her anxiety. When an elevator was moving, she always stood rigid, eyes fixated on the floor display, and when the doors finally opened, she would exhale a sigh of relief.

In the casino bar, Hannah surveyed the assortment of lushes, then sat down next to a man sipping on a nearly empty drink at the bar top. She inserted a ten-dollar bill into the video poker and played two hands, losing both. Before placing the next bet, Hannah turned to the man.

"How are you doing tonight?" she said.

The man side-eyed her before turning back to his drink. He tilted the glass and took the final sips.

"I'm sorry, sweetie. I lost my shirt on the Cowboys game, so I'm not really up for any extracurricular activities tonight. And by the looks of it, you're out of my price range."

Hannah glanced down at her attire. Hoodie, faded jeans, and weathered Converse. "You think I'm a working girl?"

"Why the hell else would a pretty girl like you be talking to an old fart like me? Or do you have a thing for overweight bald guys?"

Hannah smiled. "I was going to ask if you wanted to make a quick twenty bucks?"

The man turned and looked her over. "You wanna pay me for something? That would be a first," he slurred.

"Come on, it won't take more than a few minutes," Hannah said, grabbing his hand.

Back in the room, Hannah propped the door open using the security latch, then kicked off her shoes and sat cross-legged in the lounge chair. Carefully, she stuffed her gun into the cushion, leaving the grip hidden but accessible.

After ten minutes of waiting, she turned on the TV. *How to Win at Blackjack – Tips from a True Las Vegas Shark* was on. She watched for a few moments before lowering the volume just enough to drown out her breathing.

In a clockwise motion, she cracked her neck, then leaned forward and brought her index finger to her mouth. Meticulously, she started biting on her nails, spitting the pieces off to the side, never taking her eyes off the door.

Almost two hours after the man made the call, there was a soft knock at the door, followed by a sensual voice. "Doug, are you in here?"

Reaching behind her, she wrapped her fingers around the gun grip, practicing the motion one final time. Then she placed her hands in her lap, intertwining her fingers. Finally, in a deep voice, Hannah said, "Come in."

The girl took two steps in, saw Hannah, then stopped, and started scanning the room. Paranoia filled her eyes. Hannah couldn't tell if it was from drug abuse or fear of the unknown.

"Umm, what the fuck is going on? You don't look like a Doug to me," Marie said with trepidation.

She wore four-inch stilettos and a black sequin cocktail dress with a plunging neckline, and carried a leather clutch bag. The outfit left little to the imagination. The blond hair from the card was now red, but the eyes, nose, and lips were unmistakably the same.

Pockmarks lay strewn over her face like craters on the moon. The untrained eye might have mistaken them for the remnants of teenage acne, but Hannah knew they were most likely meth sores.

"I paid some drunk guy $20 to make the call, because I figured you wouldn't come if I did it myself."

The girl stuttered for a moment, then said, "My bodyguard is at the end of the hall, and if I'm not out of this room in an hour, he's going to kick the door in and beat the living shit out of everyone in here."

Hannah was certain that was a lie, but it didn't matter. She leaned forward, her palms facing the girl.

"I'm not going to hurt you, I promise. I just want thirty minutes of your time."

Marie looked Hannah up and down. "Just thirty minutes?"

Hannah nodded.

She rested her hand on the wall and glanced at the bed. "I mean, I've never done this before, but you're cute, so if you're going to pay, I guess I'm game."

"No, no, it's nothing like that. I just want to ask you some questions."

Confused, Marie said, "Questions about what?"

"Your time at Seven Day Saints."

"Fuck off," she said, turning toward the door.

"Please, I need your help. I'll pay you double your normal rate."

Marie stopped and looked back over her shoulder. "Help with what?"

"I'm looking for a girl who went missing, and I believe she's somewhere in Echo Canyon. Maybe being held against her will."

"Who are you? A reporter or some shit?"

"I'm a private investigator."

She took a few seconds to respond. "And how do I know Kenneth didn't send you?"

"My purse is right there," Hannah said, pointing to the bed. "Inside is my driver's license, private investigator badge, and business cards. There's also $200 in cash. You can take it and leave, or you answer some questions and get the full $400."

Cautiously, Marie approached the bed, opened the purse, and removed Hannah's wallet. She slipped the bills into her bra, then studied the driver's license.

"Colorado?"

Hannah nodded.

"How did you find me? Was it Roger?"

Reaching for the nightstand, Hannah picked up the picture Roger gave her and the escort card, holding them in front of her. "Yeah, he gave me some info and this picture. Then I collected a few hundred, or maybe a thousand of these cards, and searched them until I saw your face."

"Fuck, I knew I should've gone to Reno after I cut off communication with him," she said, slowly shaking her head. She sat on the edge of the bed, her posture tense, as if she were contemplating escape at any moment. After a few seconds, she let out a long sigh before placing her purse into her lap and opening it.

"Do you mind?" she asked, holding up a pack of Marlboro Lights.

"Be my guest."

Marie lit a cigarette and turned to Hannah. "Who are you looking for?"

"Emily Powell. She's my stepsister."

The girl thought for a moment. "The name doesn't sound familiar."

From Roger, Hannah already knew their time in Echo

Canyon wouldn't have overlapped. Marie would've been gone years before Emily ever arrived.

"I figured you didn't know her."

"So, what do you want with me?"

"I just want to learn as much as I can. Get an insider's perspective."

"And you're going to pay me $400 for this 'information'?" she said, making air quotes.

Hannah nodded. "Yes. I promise that is all I want."

She took a drag. "Fuck it, why not? It'll be the easiest money I've made in weeks."

Hannah felt a sense of ease wash over Marie, probably knowing she wouldn't have to take off her clothes to make money. Not having to worry about the countless thoughts that ran through her head every time she walked into a hotel room. Was she going to get raped? Or kidnapped? Or tortured? Or murdered?

"Do you mind if I call you Marie?"

She shimmied. "Hearing that name always gives me the willies. Since I left that fucking place, I've tried to distance myself from everything in my life during that time, including my name."

"Sorry, what would you like me to call you?"

The girl took a long drag, then tilted her head back and blew the smoke to the ceiling, watching until it disappeared.

"Since you're paying me for my time, how about you use the name my clients call me?"

"Roxy it is," Hannah said with a smile.

After a moment of silence, Roxy started tapping her watch. "Your time starts now."

Hannah grabbed a pen and notebook. "Let's start from the top. How did you end up in Echo Canyon?"

Her plan was to start with basic questions to gain her trust, then shift into difficult ones.

"My parents. They joined right before I was born."

"Okay, how did they end up there?"

"They were living in Cedar City when my mom got pregnant with me, and they weren't doing so well. Money issues, and my dad was drinking, which turned into a lot of fights. One day my mom saw a flyer on a laundromat bulletin board for a spiritual gathering put on by Seven Day Saints. She talked my dad into going, and they both swear that first night they were transformed. Finally realized their true meaning in life. Less than three months later, they packed up and moved to Echo Canyon."

"Are they still there?"

"Oh yeah. Them and my little brother. I highly doubt any of them will ever leave."

"Have you been in communication with them since you left?"

Roxy chuckled. "Are you kidding? I'll never talk to them again. In their eyes, the day I left Echo Canyon is the day I became one with the devil. Anytime anyone has ever defected, it was because they were being controlled by the dark side. That's what Kenneth preaches over and over and over again, and his word carries the weight of the world. He preaches that he's going to live forever, and I think almost everyone in town fucking believes him. I wish I could be there when he does fucking die, just to see their reaction."

Roxy turned to Hannah, and for the first time she noticed the extra layers of foundation. *Possibly an attempt to conceal a black eye?*

"Speaking of Kenneth, what do you know about that piece of shit?" Hannah said, jotting down notes.

"Where to start? Where to fucking start?" Roxy said, peering to the ceiling. "Let's see. He was an inner circle member of Seven Day, but really didn't have too much power when his father, Noah, was the leader. I think there was a lot of infighting between the two, and Kenneth was very jealous of him, but once he died—"

"How did he die?" Hannah said, cutting her off.

"In his sleep. I always heard it was natural causes."

"Was there an autopsy?"

"I doubt it. Kenneth had his funeral the next day, and he was in the ground less than twenty-four hours after dying."

"Did anyone suspect foul play?"

"If anyone did, they didn't say anything."

"Do you think Kenneth could've killed him to get control?"

"Oh yeah, he's a true psychopath, so I'd never rule out anything when it comes to him. The guy fucking married all seven of Noah's wives two days after the funeral. Not one, not two, or three, but all seven of them. All in a single afternoon, one after another, like they were waiting in line at a deli."

"And they all just went along with it? Not one of them objected?"

"Oh, I'm sure some of them didn't want to marry him, but none of them would have ever spoken those thoughts aloud."

"How many wives does he have now?"

"I don't know. Fuck, he probably doesn't know either." Roxy started counting on her fingers. "If I had to guess, I'd say at least in the thirties, and this was before I left, so I'm sure he has at least another ten more by now. It felt like whenever he got bored, he'd just marry someone new. I knew a girl who was married to a cop in Echo Canyon, and one day he came home from work and she told him she was moving out and marrying Kenneth that night."

Hannah started to feel ill. "And not one single person stands up against this fuck?"

Roxy smiled. "You really have no idea what goes on in that town, do you?"

"Oh, I'm here to learn, so please enlighten me."

She took the final drag off her cigarette, then stabbed it into the ashtray. Before the ember was out, she had lit another one.

"One of the fundamental beliefs of Seven Days Saints is that women are here on Earth for three essential reasons. One," she said, holding up her index finger, "to serve men. Two"—holding up her middle finger—"to bear children. Three"—holding up her ring finger—"to raise those children. And according to Kenneth, rule one implies that women have no choice in their own lives." Roxy shrugged. "It's all determined by Kenneth. He selects who every woman is going to marry, but the funny thing is, it doesn't even matter if someone is married because he'll sleep with whoever he wants, whenever he wants."

Roxy took another drag, then tilted her head up and exhaled a creamy cloud of smoke.

"Fuck, on my fourteenth birthday he summoned me after I had my cake and raped me. He said the only way I could become a woman was if I lay with him and gave him my virginity. I begged him not to, but nothing I said mattered." Her voice had grown hollow.

"I'm so sorry," Hannah whispered. She didn't know what else to say. Sometimes words were pointless, and this was one of those times.

Roxy shrugged. "It's life."

"No, that is not life. You were a child, and that man is a monster."

"Let me rephrase that. It's life in Echo Canyon." Roxy

took a breath. "After it happened, I needed someone to talk to, so I went to my mother and told her about what he did. And as I cried in her arms, do you know what she told me?"

"I don't know, but I'm sure it's going to make me sick," Hannah said, dropping the pen onto the notepad.

"That it was her idea, and I should feel special, feel honored. Kenneth selected me, out of all the girls in Echo Canyon. Not everyone is worthy of relations with the leader, and I was."

"I can't believe your own fucking mother gave you to him," Hannah said, choking on the words.

"That night, I truly realized my mother was gone, and there was no saving her. I was a chess piece in her game to get in Kenneth's good grace." Roxy cleared her throat. "After that night, Kenneth called me to his room about once a month, and around the fifth or sixth time, I just closed my eyes and imagined I was far, far away."

Hannah had expected that Roxy would weave horror stories, but these were far worse than she had anticipated. Kenneth was in the ranks of some of the worst—Manson, Koresh, Jones.

"A few weeks after my sixteenth birthday, Kenneth sat me down in his room, and told me I was going to marry a man named Jared Evans. He was the treasurer for Seven Day, and one of the men in Kenneth's inner circle. I probably never said more than a few words to the man, and they wanted me to marry him."

"What would've happened if you refused?"

"I did. I told him, 'I'm not going to marry that man,' and the look in his eyes is something I'll never forget. I thought he was going to kill me right there. He just stared at me for a long time, minutes maybe, never moving, barely blinking, then patted my thigh and said, 'Come on, I want to show you something.' That's when he took me to the Healing Room." Roxy let out a long sigh.

"I'm guessing it isn't a place for spiritual reflection."

"No, it's closer to solitary confinement. Imagine a tiny, windowless room with a bed and a couple of chairs, and an even smaller bathroom that only has a toilet and sink. It's only accessible from a hidden door in one of the offices, and unless you knew it was there, you'd never find it. Kenneth kept me down there until I agreed to marry Jared. I was only down there for five days, but it felt like months."

Roxy glanced at the ceiling and ran her hand through her hair a few times.

"The ceremony was small. Me, Jared, Kenneth as the minister, and my mother and father. I cried the entire time, and none of them batted an eye. My mother thought they were tears of happiness. I'd never kissed that piece of shit, or even held his hand before our wedding. Then hours after we were married, I was being raped by him."

Fury coursed through Hannah's body. Kenneth and everyone who was complicit needed to be burned at the stake.

"After the ceremony, I learned he was fucking forty-three years old. I was a teenager, a kid, and this fucking man ... this piece of shit was already middle-aged. I was his fifth wife, and two more came within a year. He had eight children, two of them older than me, and one was even in my class." Roxy forced a smile. "And even after I was married, Kenneth would still request I come to his room about once a week. Six months after the wedding, I was pregnant."

"Do you know who the father is?"

"As horrible a person as Jared is, I pray that those kids are not Kenneth's," Roxy said with misery all over her face.

"Kids?" Hannah said.

The girl's eyes locked on the door like she was considering bolting. After a few seconds, she turned back to Hannah.

"Yes, I have two. Oliver is eight, and Clara turns seven next week. I'm sure Kenneth is already grooming her. I have nightmares of what's going to happen." She paused. "And I know what you're probably thinking. How could I just leave my children with those monsters?"

Hannah was indeed thinking that, but she would never have uttered the words.

"Well, since I questioned Kenneth's ideologies, I was considered dangerous, so as a punishment, they were both taken away and handed over to one of Kenneth's wives. They used me as an example of what would happen if you defied them."

"Are they still in Echo Canyon?"

"Maybe. I don't know for sure. About a year before I left, they were just gone one day. I think they were moved to either Alberta or Mexico. Nobody would tell me. I begged Jared, punching him in the chest, but he just grabbed my wrists and threw me to the ground. Then he knelt and whispered, 'They're both alive and well, and you'll never see them or hold them again.' That was my breaking point. On most days after that, I wished I was dead. Fantasizing about running a knife over my wrists, or jumping in front of a car," Roxy said, fighting back tears.

Hannah's anxiety swelled as she imagined herself in that situation. The choice, right or wrong, would've been easy—she would've killed Jared and herself long before giving birth.

"One day, I decided I'd had enough, and I climbed up a ridge outside of town. I sat on the edge and stared down to the canyon floor. Then I got up and hovered on one foot, swaying back and forth. But something inside me said don't do it, and I just lowered my foot, and sat back down. I decided right there I wasn't going to let them defeat me."

"Did you ever report any of this once you left?"

"You're joking right? That place is untouchable."

"No place is."

"They are."

"What about the raid in '92?"

"You're kidding, right? You wanna call that a raid? That was more of a performance than anything. Everyone in town knew the FBI were coming for almost an entire week, like someone posted it on the front page of the paper. They walked away with nothing, and Kenneth was able to preach that the community was protected from someone from above." Roxy shook her head. "Then, after the fuck-up in Ruby Ridge and the Branch Davidian compound, I don't think any government agency will set foot in Echo Canyon unless they have a mountain of evidence."

A loud scream interrupted them, but Hannah couldn't place where it was coming from. Next door, or across the hall, or a story up or a story down. She leaned forward to listen better, and after a few moments, she realized it was someone having sex. Roxy didn't acknowledge the sound. Probably white noise to her, hearing screams like that multiple times a night.

Hannah leaned back and tapped the pen on the notepad. "Coming from an outsider, what I still can't comprehend is how a grown adult can blindly follow every one of his orders."

"Simple. He uses fear. Fear of the unknown, fear of living, and fear of dying. If he asked the town to walk over the rim of the canyon and plummet to their death, most of them probably would. He preaches that when the end of the world comes, cities and countries will be destroyed and millions will perish, and the only city that will remain is Echo Canyon, and it will be the birthplace of the new world. And anyone that defies his beliefs will be the first to die and will spend a thousand years in complete darkness."

"And no one wants to spend a thousand years in darkness," Hannah said sarcastically.

Roxy nodded. "Even if they think all the end-of-the-world talk is bullshit, they are fearful of what Kenneth can do to them—he can take away your children, your husband or your wife. He can bankrupt you, or get you fired, or evict you from your house, or banish you from the community. Simply put, he can ruin your life, all with the snap of his fingers. That is why almost no one ever leaves."

"But you had the strength to leave," Hannah said.

Roxy attempted a smile. "Yes, and I'm sure after I vanished, he preached that I was a whore and I'd spend eternity in hell, you know, all that jazz."

"If there is a hell, I'm pretty certain I know who is going, and it's not going to be you." Hannah grabbed a bottle of Jack Daniel's. She took a slug, then offered it to Roxy.

"I try not to drink when I'm working."

Hannah placed the bottle on the floor, then flipped to a new page in the notepad. "Do they have weapons?"

"They have an arsenal big enough to start a small war, and it looks like they're stockpiling for one, but they go to extreme measures to conceal them. When I was there, there was a very strict rule that Kenneth's guards were the only people allowed to carry a gun."

"He has guards? That is the first I'm hearing of that."

"Oh yeah, he's so fucking paranoid because his brain is mush from the booze and pills and blow, and he believes people are trying to kill him, so the second he steps foot outside the compound, his guards are like his shadow."

"I thought drugs and alcohol were forbidden in Echo Canyon."

"They are for the common folk, but Kenneth and the inner circle members have access to anything they want. Pills, booze, you name it. Almost every night I was with him, he'd drink a bottle of wine, then do a few lines of blow, and like an hour later he'd pop two or three Valium."

"And he could function on all that?"

"No." Roxy chuckled. "He couldn't get hard the last few times I was with him. I mean, he was falling apart before I left, so I couldn't imagine how bad he is now."

"So, the powerful, self-proclaimed leader has ED problems?"

Roxy snorted. "Yes, very much so."

"Just out of curiosity, how did you escape?"

"That'd take all night."

"I've got the time."

Roxy glanced at her watch. "No, you don't. Your time is almost up, so I'll give you the condensed version." She cracked her neck and lit another cigarette. "I was friends with this guy Chuck. We met in fourth grade, and he's pretty much the only friend I've ever had. As we got older, we confided in each other about almost everything. I'd tell him what was happening with Kenneth, and Jared, and after some time he told me he was gay."

"I'm guessing if someone found out, he'd be shipped off to some sort of conversion therapy."

"Probably worse. According to Kenneth, being gay is the worst sin a man can commit. Chuck lived in utter fear that one day, someone would come to his door and take him away." Roxy stopped for a moment and wiped her eyes with the back of her hand. "When we were alone, we always talked about how we wanted to escape. He promised he'd never leave me, and I promised the same. After I told him about wanting to jump off the cliff, he grabbed me by the shoulders and said, 'We are getting the fuck out of here.' We started brainstorming a bunch of dumb ideas like stealing a car, hiking out, starting the compound on fire. Then one day, like someone granted our wish, our names got called to make a run to St. George."

"Run to St. George?"

"Yeah, like twice a month, they send people for supplies. Walmart, Costco, grocery store—places like that. It's always two or three people. I went a few times, and I think Chuck said he went at least a dozen, but that was the first time our names were called together. As we sat in the van, we thought for sure it was a setup, but when we made it to the highway, we knew they had no idea."

"So did you just keep driving past St. George?" Hannah said.

"Yeah. We stopped for gas, then drove north to Salt Lake, then west on I-80, toward Reno. A couple of times during the drive, I thought I was going to pee my pants, but we didn't want to make any unnecessary stops. We were so scared, but we kept telling ourselves that it'd be almost impossible for them to catch us because we had at least a three-hour head start. Then, after driving almost twelve hours, we saw the lights of Reno on the horizon. I'd never seen anything like it. It was like I was in a different world."

"What did you do when you got to Reno?"

"We slept in a bus station parking lot, and in the morning, we went to a diner for breakfast. He gave me $500, half the money for the Walmart run, the rest he'd secretly been stashing. He told me to get a bus ticket to somewhere far, but he didn't want to know where. It'd be safer for both of us if we didn't know where the other one was going. That was the longest goodbye of my life. I think I cried for a solid twenty minutes. Then he got in the van and drove away. I stood there like a dummy hoping he'd turn around, but he never did."

"Have you talked to him since?"

"Nope. I have no idea where he is. If he's still alive, or if Seven Day found him and took him back to Echo Canyon."

"What did you do after he left? And how did you end up in Vegas?"

Roxy stabbed the cigarette into the ashtray, then smiled and shook her head. "Not tonight."

"Fine, but do you feel safe here? I mean, Vegas is only two, three hours from Echo Canyon."

"I actually do. It's Sin City, and I don't think anyone from Echo Canyon would come within a twenty-mile radius."

Roxy picked up a can of Coke off the nightstand and rotated it. "Wanna hear something crazy? I never had a Coke when I lived there. Not a single soda. It was a fucking culture shock leaving that place." She lifted the can to her mouth, took a large gulp, then gently placed it down.

"I bet."

"There are some fucking freaks that hire me, stuff that if you saw in a movie, you'd think it was fake, but nope, men actually pay me for. Like this guy last week, he calls me to the penthouse in the Bellagio. This room was like a palace, probably one of the biggest ones in the entire hotel.

"Well, I show up, he greets me, takes my coat, and gives me a tour. Very nice guy, very polite. He probably was in his sixties, decent looking for his age, I guess. I picture this guy is married, and on a business trip, and wants to get lucky while he's in Vegas. It's happened more times than I can count. Most of the time, these types of guys are pretty basic. Missionary, with a condom, and they cum within a few minutes, then roll over, maybe cry, then tell me where the money is and ask me to leave."

Hannah had been an investigator long enough to know when to ask questions and when to listen. This was a time to listen.

"Well, this guy offers me a glass of wine. I told him I don't drink on the job, but he was persistent, so I finally said yes. He pours two glasses, then proceeds to tell me about the wine. I don't know if he was bullshitting, but he said it was a rare 1920s bottle from the south of France, something about the grapes. I pretended like I cared, but I'm thinking shut up and fuck me already because I want to go home."

"I'm guessing this guy wanted something besides the good old missionary position."

"Yeah. When we finish the bottle, he lays out five $100 bills on the table. Then, with a straight face, he says he wants me to lube the bottle up, then stick it up his ass while he jerks off. My jaw dropped to the ground."

"Did you do it?"

"I mean, $500 is $500. When he finished, he took the bottle, wiped it off with a towel, and placed it back on the table and stared at it like it was a trophy or something." Roxy laughed to herself. "And do you wanna hear the best part?"

Hannah nodded. "Of course I do."

"I see this dude on TV like a month later. That fucker is one of the top guys with the Nevada Gaming Commission. He was doing a local news interview with his wife, talking about his kids. I just pointed at the TV and laughed. If they only knew."

Roxy took a drag and blew the smoke out of the side of her mouth. "But as disgusting as that sounds, I'd rather stick a bottle in some guy's ass every night for the rest of my life than have to touch Kenneth again." She stood up. "I wanna show you something."

Roxy lifted her dress a couple of inches. On her inner left thigh, about three inches below her hip, was a large, square bandage. After a quick, deep breath, she ripped it off.

"Fuck, that stung." She grimaced.

Seared into her flesh were the letters SDS. "Seven. Day. Saints," Roxy said, tapping each letter.

"He fucking branded you," Hannah said.

"According to Kenneth, the brand is required to become a true woman, and once you have this marking, he is yours forever." She didn't take her eyes off the scar. "I have to wear a bandage almost every day. Anytime I work, or anytime I wear a bikini, or a short skirt, all because of that fucking piece of shit."

Roxy lowered her dress, hiding the scar. "For a long time, I thought about going to a plastic surgeon and getting it removed, or just taking a razor blade and removing it myself, but I said fuck it, I don't want it gone, because every time I look in the mirror, I'm reminded that I'll never go back. Never." She glanced down. "Your time is up."

Leaning back in her chair, Hannah tossed the notepad onto the floor. "Can I ask one last question?"

"Yeah, I'll let you have a freebie."

"Do you really have a bodyguard down the hall?"

Roxy looked at Hannah for a moment, then turned away. "No. I probably could be gone for days before anyone knew I was missing. Are you really looking for your sister?"

"Yeah, my stepsister."

A long silence followed. Then Roxy said, "Well, I hope you find her." She smiled, blew a kiss, and slipped out the door, closing it softly behind her.

When Hannah arrived at Roger's trailer, he was sitting on the porch, tossing a weathered tennis ball to Kona. The dog casually walked across the yard, picked up the ball, then dropped it at his feet before sitting next to the chair, staring up as if begging him not to throw it again.

"If I didn't make her come outside, she'd pretty much do nothing but sleep and eat," Roger said.

"I hear they're quite the couch potatoes."

"Yes indeed."

Roger massaged Kona's head for a moment, then placed the ball in a basket and told her to lie down. Kona curled up at his feet. Roger leaned back in the chair and folded his arms, resting them on his belly.

"Did you find her?"

Hannah nodded. "I only had to walk the length of the strip about ten times and talk to a few hundred drunks, pimps, and prostitutes, but I found her."

She took a seat next to Roger and told him everything from her conversation with Roxy. After she finished, he remained silent, scratching his chin the entire time.

"So, hypothetical question for you," Hannah said.

"Please don't say what I think you're about to say," Roger said.

"And remember, this is hypothetical, but if someone wanted to go to Echo Canyon. What would you suggest?"

"I'd suggest they go to the hospital and get their head checked out."

"Come on, I'm being serious."

He looked at her, eyebrows raised. "After everything I told you, and everything you just told me, you still think that it's a smart idea?"

"Oh, I don't think it is a smart idea, but I have to try to

find Emily and see if she's alive and okay. I'm not going to be able to live with myself if I don't go there and at least try. And if I find evidence that could lock up Kenneth, well that would be icing on the cake."

"So, do you think you're just going to stroll into town, snoop around until you find Emily, then take her home?"

"That'd be ideal," she said with a smirk.

Roger glared at her like a father being stern with his daughter. Then he removed a toothpick from his front pocket and placed it in his mouth. "If they have an inkling who you are, you're toast."

"Don't worry, I'm just going to get a room and then spend a few days investigating. If I get a feeling something's wrong, I'll get the hell out of there."

Roger let out a heavy sigh.

"I'll be fine, I promise." She took a moment. "I mean, this is still America, and they can't kidnap me and throw me in some dungeon and lock me away forever for asking questions. Right?"

Hannah wasn't entirely certain about the last statement, but saying it aloud calmed her nerves.

"I wouldn't put anything past them."

"Umm, I was kinda hoping you'd give me some reassurance. Like, 'You'll be okay, just don't do anything stupid,' then I'd say, 'I can't promise that, because I tend to veer toward stupid,' then we'd both laugh."

Tight-lipped, Roger shook his head. "You know if you get in trouble, I won't be able to help you."

"I know."

Kona stood up and shook her head, then lay between Hannah's feet and looked up at her, like she was pleading with Hannah not to go either, but her mind was already set.

"Any chance I could get the number to that reporter from the *Salt Lake Times*?"

Roger went inside. A few minutes later, he returned and handed Hannah a torn piece of paper with a name and number scribbled on it.

"Any last words of advice?" Hannah said, slipping the paper into her pocket.

"From the sounds of it, you know as much as I do about Echo Canyon, if not more, so I don't have any words of wisdom, but I will say it one more time: they are very dangerous. Don't ever forget that, and don't ever let your guard down."

Hannah started to stand but quickly sat back down. She slipped off her necklace and held it out to him.

"What are you doing with that?" he said.

"It's my sister's, and I don't want anything to happen to it." Hannah stared at the necklace. "It means more than anything in the world to me."

"And you want me to take it?"

"More like storing it. Just in case anything goes sideways. I don't want even the slightest chance that something could happen to it."

Roger nodded. "It'll be in safe keeping, and I'll return it the moment you get back, so don't go getting yourself killed."

"I'll try not to."

FIVE

S t. George Used Auto was the kind of dealership where people with bad credit went to buy cars. The vehicles were probably purchased from an auction, or they were salvageable wrecks, or repos, or from someone in a bind who needed money more than they needed transportation.

Hannah eyed an early '90s Camry. It was one of the only cars under $2,000 that also didn't look like the wheels would fall off the moment she drove off the lot. It wasn't an ideal pick, but it'd do in a pinch.

A salesman spotted her from across the lot and waved. The list of things she'd rather do than talk to a used car salesman included getting a mammogram and going to a country concert. They preyed on the poor and uneducated. Her goal was to complete the transaction as fast as possible, with the least amount of conversation.

As he approached, he smiled, revealing his coffee and smoke-stained teeth. The smell of cheap aftershave was overwhelming, and it was a poor attempt at covering foul body odor.

"How are you doing today, sweetheart?"

She despised anyone other than her dad or significant other calling her sweetheart. She glared for a moment, then faked a smile.

"I'm interested in this beauty," she said, kicking a tire on the Camry.

At first, Hannah had been planning to drive her own car to Echo Canyon, but if someone from Seven Day Saints *was* watching Roger's house, they would've seen her and the vehicle she drove. Bad idea. Then, she contemplated getting a rental, but that required a credit card, so it would be a lot faster to trace back to her. Better, but still not the best solution. So, she decided to purchase a used car, paying with cash. Paperwork would usually take at least a few days to file, and longer on the weekend, and hopefully she'd be far away from Echo Canyon by the time anyone outside of the dealership knew it was registered to her.

It was probably overly cautious, but she preferred the safe approach. Drive the clunker for a few days, then when she returned from Echo Canyon, she'd sell it back to the dealership, probably for half of what she paid. At the end of the day, keeping her identity hidden was worth the money.

The salesmen looked her up and down, presumably gauging her knowledge of cars and if she knew the difference between a dipstick and a piston.

"This is a solid car. I was thinking about getting it for my mother," he said.

Hannah glared at him again, and this time she held the gaze long enough to make him feel uncomfortable.

"Let me rephrase. I want to buy this car, but I have two requests, and I don't want to hear your cheesy sales lines, like how it was only driven to church on Sundays by some grandma."

He let out a subtle cough. "Sure, let's hear them."

"One, you need to throw on a new pair of front tires—these guys almost have the steel belts showing. Two, I need a place to park my other car. Probably a couple days, maybe a week at the most."

"You're paying sticker price?"

Hannah nodded. "Yeah, cash."

"Yeah, I think I can accommodate those requests," he said, twisting his mustache.

"One more thing—I'm only buying it if that CD player works."

Some two hours later, Hannah was driving east on Highway 99 in her newly purchased Camry. The alignment was off, and the car kept pulling toward oncoming traffic. Multiple speakers were blown, and a strange scent emanated from the backseat, an unpleasant combination of cigarettes and fast food. Maybe when she returned from Echo Canyon, she'd drive it off a cliff and put it out of its misery.

About ten miles outside of St. George, she turned down a dirt road, drove for about a half mile, then made a U-turn. She put the car in park, grabbed her backpack, and walked to the trunk of the car.

In the backpack was a license plate she'd removed off a wrecked Dodge Caravan in an abandoned gas station shortly after leaving Cortez. Colorado plates would add an additional layer of difficulty for anyone in Utah attempting to identify the vehicle, another precaution to conceal her identity. She hid the temporary plates next to the bald spare tire, then climbed back into the car and turned back onto the highway.

The lack of any trees troubled Hannah. For all its beauty, some parts of Utah resembled the surface of another planet.

Multiple times, she reached down for Casey's necklace, only to remember she'd given it to Roger for safekeeping. She felt naked without it. It was her good luck charm. It might as well have been her Xanax. Each time, she wished it was around her neck, but she knew leaving it with Roger had been the smart decision. If something happened to her, the necklace would be given to her father instead of falling into the hands of someone else.

As she was fighting to keep her eyes open, it started to rain. Turning off the stereo, Hannah listened to the pat-pat splatter of raindrops onto the car. It was soothing at first, but within a few minutes she was forced to turn the wipers from medium to the highest setting. They were useless.

The storm raged, and the raindrops grew larger and louder, hitting the car as if pelting it with pebbles, and with each passing mile, the visibility lessened. Water began rushing over the highway, almost obscuring the pavement, and for a minute she feared she'd missed the signs stating that this section of the highway was a flash flood zone. The Camry was no match for a few inches of rushing water. The car would be swept away like a feather and carried into the high desert.

And then, like someone flipped a switch, the rain stopped. The clouds dissipated and sunlight shone into the valley, drying the road within minutes.

Red Mesa sat at the junction of Highway 99 and 289, forty miles northeast of Echo Canyon, and almost three hundred miles to Salt Lake City as the crow flies. Just like most of the towns Hannah drove through on 99, it was nothing more than a main street with a couple of motels, a handful of restaurants, and one or two gas stations. If she hadn't been staying in town, she would've driven right through and probably never thought twice about it.

Hannah got a room at the Big Horn Inn, then unpacked her bag, carefully placing everything on the right side of the bed. Three shirts, two pairs of jeans, four pairs of socks—two unmatched—and three pairs of underwear.

"Three days," she whispered. "Okay, four days, but that is it."

She picked up the remote then aimlessly flipped through the channels, stopping on a Salt Lake City news station. She watched for a few minutes, a local segment about a charity event for a family whose house burned down.

Hannah pressed mute, then slipped her hand into her pocket and removed the paper with the number of the *Salt Lake Times* reporter. Over the last three days, she'd called six times with no answer and no option to leave a message. She'd come to three conclusions about why the calls were going unanswered. Either it was a wrong number, the reporter had moved and hadn't forwarded his number, or he was screening his calls, not answering unknown numbers.

Hannah picked up the phone and dialed again. This time, after three rings, a man's voice said, "Hello?" almost liked he'd answered by mistake.

"Is this Rex Ward from the *Salt Lake Times?*"

"It is, who's calling?"

Hannah sprang up on the bed, almost dropping the receiver. Talking at double speed, she introduced herself and where she got his number, then said, "I'm wondering if I could ask you some questions about Echo Canyon."

A brief pause followed before he spoke. "Umm, could I give you a call back in like fifteen minutes? I'm right in the middle of making dinner."

"Sure," Hannah said, then provided him with a callback number.

After Hannah hung up, she grabbed a deck of cards out of her backpack. She shuffled four times and dealt out a hand of solitaire. After about every third draw, she glanced at the phone, and with each losing hand, her hope of speaking to Rex faded.

In the middle of the sixth game, the phone finally rang. "Rex?" Hannah murmured.

"Yes, sorry about that, I don't feel comfortable talking about Echo Canyon on my home phone, so I went to the gas station across the street and called from a pay phone."

"Do you think your phone is tapped?"

"I don't think so. Well, I guess I don't know. I mean, sometimes I'll be on a call and hear these clicking sounds that I never heard before I worked on the story. I thought it was my phone, so I bought a new one, and the clicks are still there." His voice was shaky, and she could sense the paranoia in every word. "And like a few times a week, someone rings my doorbell, but when I answer, no one is there."

"So, you think Seven Day Saints is ding-dong ditching you? From what I've heard, that really doesn't seem like their style."

"I know it sounds dumb, but that never happened either. And I swear I'm being followed sometimes. I know it has to be them."

"No, it's not dumb, it just seems a little childish. I feel like if they wanted to scare you, they'd be a little more intimidating." Hannah lit a cigarette and took a quick drag. "Have you heard about Roger's dog?"

"Yeah, luckily I don't have any pets."

"Lucky you," Hannah said with a touch of sarcasm.

"Hannah, it's like thirty degrees out and I forgot my coat, so could we get to the reason for your call?"

"I'm on my way to Echo Canyon, and I've only talked to two people who have been there. One is Marie, and she's been gone for years, and the other, I don't know how much I trust him, so I wanted to talk to someone who's been there somewhat recently."

"First off, is there any way I could talk you out of going?"

"You're going to have to get in line."

"I take it I'm already late?"

"I'm sitting in my room in Red Mesa right now, so yeah."

"Fuck, alright. I guess I'll start with, I had no idea what I was expecting when I got there. I mean, I had never heard of Echo Canyon or Seven Day Saints before talking to Marie, but I'd say for a community that has a motto of 'Love Thy Brother and Sister,' they are not very friendly to outsiders."

"If you didn't know about Echo Canyon, how did you find Marie?"

"I didn't. She contacted me after she read the story I wrote on Kelly Wright."

Hannah remembered almost every detail about the Kelly Wright abduction. She was sixteen when she was taken from a bus stop in Provo, Utah, while on the way to her job as a lifeguard at a local pool. The missing person search party was one of the largest in Utah's history, with a reward that reached $100,000 within the first week.

Kelly's face was on the front page of countless newspapers and the lead story on local and national stations.

The initial suspect was Carlos Garcia, an undocumented thirty-three-year-old landscaper from Juarez, Mexico. He'd worked on the Wright property, and Kelly's little sister, Amber, had told police that she'd seen him staring at Kelly in a way that made her feel uncomfortable. After twenty hours of interrogation, he was released due to lack of evidence and a solid alibi, but INS was waiting, and he was deported back to Mexico.

Eleven days after the abduction, an alert gas attendant in Eugene, Oregon, recognized Kelly and called police. The man accompanying Kelly entered the store, and the attendant stalled by saying the cash register wasn't working. When police arrived, the man escaped out the back door, but he was apprehended five blocks away.

For the first twenty minutes, Kelly denied her identity, saying her name was Robin and the man was her uncle. When the investigator placed Kelly's father on speaker phone, she broke down and admitted she was Kelly. The man had threatened that if she ever spoke her birth name again, he was going to kill her entire family.

The abductor was a thirty-seven-year-old white male named Carl Webb. He was an unemployed house painter who lived alone and was weeks away from getting evicted. After he saw Kelly at the pool, he'd become infatuated with her. A suitcase found in the car contained countless pictures of her, and there were numerous journals detailing a fictional romance where he was her knight in shining armor.

While in custody, Carl never spoke a word, even to his lawyers. The night before his arraignment, he hung himself with a bedsheet.

"I was captivated by that story," Hannah said. "I read everything I could on it, so I might've come across your piece."

"It's by far the best work I've ever done. I mean, I won a Pulitzer for it." He paused for a moment. "Well, it was until my story on Echo Canyon. When Marie called, she said it was going to be a hundred times bigger, and she was right."

"If it'd only gone to print," Hannah said.

"If only. So, Echo Canyon. I'll start by saying only one out of four of my sources had ever heard of it or Seven Day Saints. And these are not your run-of-the-mill investigators, these guys are pros, and specialize in finding people who don't want to be found. And the guy that had heard of it thought they were just a Mormon fundamentalist group."

Rex started with the financial details of Echo Canyon, which were of no interest to Hannah, but she didn't want to interrupt and disrupt the conversation.

"Annually, the residents of Echo Canyon receive millions of dollars of government assistance. Ten times more than all other Utah residents. For every dollar they pay in taxes, they receive ten in return. Any idea why?"

"If I had to guess, I'd say because of plural marriage."

"Bingo. On paper, the majority of the women in Echo Canyon state they are single, but they all have multiple children. And when I say multiple, I mean four or five. Fuck, I found one lady who had twelve kids and had never had a job before."

"Her job is to get pregnant," Hannah said.

"Exactly. These people believe the government is pure evil, but don't shy away from taking any government assistance they can get."

"Sounds like a nice racket to keep money flowing to Mr. Pratt."

"Yes, it is."

Rex spent the next ten minutes recounting his time in Echo Canyon, detailing the people, the town, and his insights on the compound, but nothing he said would help Hannah locate Emily. At one point, he had to insert a few more quarters.

"Maybe you'll have better luck than me since you're a woman, but almost everyone I talked to didn't say more than a few words to me. Almost like they were following orders."

"I'm sure they were," Hannah said.

"Yes. I had a feeling they knew I was coming from a mile away."

"Do you suspect that someone from your paper told Kenneth?"

"I'd bet my last ten dollars on it." Rex paused. "If I were you, I'd always be cognizant that your room is bugged, your phone is tapped, and they will be following your every movement. Before I went, I bought this bug detector from a surveillance store in Salt Lake, and I found three bugs in my room. Three, and that was with a cheap detector. I guarantee there was more. Fuck, those were probably the ones they wanted me to find. I'd say, to be on the safe side, even when you're alone, don't say anything you don't want them to hear."

"You make it sound like North Korea."

"I know a reporter who's been there, and from what he told me, some of the similarities are uncanny. Can I tell you something off the record?"

"Yes, of course."

"You're not going to— I mean, you can't repeat this, because it could put this person's life in danger."

"Trust me, I won't," Hannah said, her voice tight.

"On my third day, I was having lunch at this place

called Echo Cafe, and the waitress was this sweet girl. By my best guess, she couldn't have been older than sixteen, but I don't know, now that I'm on the other side of forty, it's hard for me to tell if someone is fourteen or twenty-four. Well, after I finished my lunch, she gave me a free slice of bumbleberry pie."

"I don't think you needed to go off the record to tell me about a piece of pie."

"I'm not telling you this because of the pie, I'm telling you about the girl. She said her name was Anna, but who knows if that was her real name. We had a nice conversation about a hike I did in Alaska, and well, when she dropped off my check, there was a folded-up piece of paper underneath it. She looked back to the kitchen, probably to make sure no one was watching, then turned back to me and winked. I slipped it into my pocket, paid the check, then casually walked to the motel. I locked the doors, turned on the TV, and climbed under the sheets."

"Under the sheets?" Hannah muttered.

"Yeah, like I said, I was paranoid that they might have hidden cameras in the room. Well, when I opened the note, it simply read, 'You're in danger, leave immediately.' I read it like five times before it fully processed, and then this feeling of dread washed over me. I've covered stories in Iraq, so I've seen some shit, but this was something entirely different."

"Do you think this girl was genuine, or just trying to scare you enough to leave?"

"I've interviewed hundreds of people, and I know when someone is lying. I'm almost certain she was telling the truth."

"So, what did you do after you read the note?"

"What do you think? I tossed everything in my suitcase and got the fuck out of there. I was in such a hurry, I forgot a pair of glasses on the bathroom sink."

"I'm sure if you called, they would've sent them to you."

"Not funny, Hannah. Not one bit. I truly think this girl was trying to save me from something. I don't know what, but the look in her eyes told me that I was in serious trouble."

"Well, the town isn't completely evil like I've been told."

"Yeah, there's at least one good person. A needle in a haystack," he said, trailing off. The line was silent for ten seconds, then Rex said, "Are you really going?"

"Yeah, I'm leaving tomorrow morning."

"Well, remember, don't trust anyone."

That wouldn't be hard for Hannah. It was how she'd lived most of her adult life.

"No one, huh? What about the waitress?"

"Nope. I have no idea why she seemingly helped me, and who knows if she'd do it for you. Maybe it was her one good deed for the year. Or maybe someone at Seven Day found out, and she's been exiled. If I were you, I'd assume everything I did was being reported back to Kenneth and the inner circle."

After checking the door handle three times, Hannah looked down the walkway. At the end, an old man sat in a plastic lawn chair, probably as old as the motel itself, systematically bringing a cigarette to his mouth every twenty seconds, like he was on a timer. Hannah waved, and he nodded begrudgingly. She turned back and started across the parking lot toward Highway 99.

As she walked, a low, milky fog hung in the air, limiting visibility to a few hundred feet, obscuring anything beyond

Red Mesa. Within five minutes, a light snow began to fall, the type of snow that turns from a flake into a raindrop before it reaches the ground. The fog and the dusting insulated the night, and almost every sound was deadened.

Only two restaurants were open, both taverns, and the menus in the guest directory in her room were nearly identical. Mostly burgers and pizza. They were both a half-mile walk from the motel, located directly across the highway from each other.

Hannah picked the Antelope Saloon, simply due to the fact it was on the side of the road she was already on. When she got there, she ordered a BBQ burger and fries, medium well. She didn't consume red meat often, but on the occasions when she did, it had to be fully cooked—the thought of biting into anything still bleeding turned her stomach.

Along with the burger, she drank two Coors Lights and had two shots of Jack Daniel's. Briefly, she considered getting a third shot, but she was already feeling somewhat tipsy, so she decided against it.

On the walk back to the motel, Hannah stopped at the junction of Highway 99 and 289, staring at the pavement heading due south. A mileage sign for Echo Canyon stood riddled with small gunshot holes. Maybe a final warning to turn back.

When she arrived back at the motel, the old man was still smoking on the walkway. His face was long, and his movements were deliberate, like he didn't want to waste any unnecessary energy.

Peering down, Hannah noticed an oxygen tank on the ground next to his chair and a cannula running from the tank to his nostrils. The man took a drag, then rested his arm, cigarette in hand, mere inches from the tank.

On the side of the tank was a large "Oxygen in Use –

No Smoking" sticker. After foreseeing the explosion that could occur if the pure oxygen came into contact with the ember, something that would likely obliterate the man and probably take out a few of Hannah's limbs, she took three large steps back.

"It's pretty cold out," Hannah said, cringing as the words escaped her mouth. The night was frigid, a cold she had never experienced in Colorado. If a doctor told her icicles had already formed in her lungs, she would've believed them.

The man glanced up, blew out a cloud of smoke, and nodded. "Sure is."

Hannah decided to skip the small talk. "Are you from this area?"

The man stared at Hannah for a moment, then raised his arm and pointed across the street.

"I was born about two blocks south of here. Back in those days, women around here didn't go to the hospital, they gave birth in the bathtub."

Hannah smiled. "Random question, but have you ever heard of a man named Kenneth Pratt?" The words felt rehearsed.

"Most people that stay here don't be asking about the Pratts."

"I'm not most people. I'm an investigator looking for a missing girl."

"I see," the man said, looking Hannah over from head to toe.

"So, do you know him?"

"Nah, I never met him, but I knew his daddy."

"Anything you want to share?"

"Lady, you don't wanna hear what I've done."

"Yes, I do."

The man leaned forward and looked to the left, then

right, like he was worried that someone would step out of a room and overhear their conversation.

"No one is going to hear what you say, and I can promise you that your secret is safe with me."

He let out a long sigh. "Fuck it, I'm going to be dead in the few months, so there's nothing anyone can do to me now. And who knows, maybe telling you will buy me some goodwill with the man upstairs."

For some reason, people opened up to Hannah without knowing her true motives. Maybe it was her sweet smile or her kind eyes. Or maybe she had a way of asking the right questions. Whatever the reason, it was a valuable asset in her line of profession.

After a final drag, he flicked the cigarette into the parking lot. "I did a bunch of work for Noah back in the seventies. Drywall, painting, odd job stuff. When I started, he paid me at the end of the day, but the more work I did, the larger I allowed the bill to grow. Well, after this big project, he owed me almost $1,000. He tells me that he didn't have the money to pay the full amount, so he offers me a deal."

Hannah had a hunch she already knew the answer, but she blurted out the words. "What type of deal?"

"He, umm, takes me to his room, and there are five girls sitting on the bed, and he told me I could pick one."

"And you picked a girl?" Hannah muttered.

"I was in a very dark place back then. My demons controlled me. I was never faithful, and did my best to be a good man, but I was too weak to say no to Noah's offer." The man cleared his throat, coughed, then spat out something more red than green. "I didn't want to, I swear I didn't, but there was something inside me that forced me to do it."

Speechless, Hannah looked away from the man,

mustering every ounce of strength to hide her disgust. How could a man rape and destroy an innocent girl just for his own pleasure? No jail time was long enough, no punishment too harsh. Hell, she would be fine with castration and bleeding out to death.

He turned and spat again, waiting for Hannah to say something, but she didn't, so he continued.

"The last time I was there, he gave me a girl who could not have been more than fifteen. I swear to you, I wanted to say no, but in the moment, I just couldn't stop myself." The man glanced up to the sky, his face weary, eyes glazed over. "Well, she was crying the entire time, and when I finished, I realized I was a monster. Right then, I made a promise that I'd never go back. The entire drive home, I told myself if I ever get tempted to, I'll put a damn shotgun in my mouth."

Hearing him admit his sins gave Hannah little faith in humanity. In no world could she comprehend anyone capable of such heinous acts.

"When I was driving home, my wife Betsy and my daughters Mary and Julie were driving back from Christmas shopping in St. George. I was supposed to be with them, but I lied and told them I had to do some work in Echo Canyon," he said, his voice dropping.

The man looked at Hannah with a lifetime of regret in his eyes. Then, in a steady rhythm, he began tapping his boot on the weathered wood planks.

"About five miles from our house, a couple of drunk high school kids veered over the center line and crashed head-on into them. Betsy and Mary died on impact, but Julie, my youngest, survived for almost a month until she passed. I held her hand every night, and prayed, and prayed, and prayed for forgiveness, but the lord took her. I died that very night."

"That's terrible," Hannah whispered, thinking how it should've been him who perished in that collision.

"I've replayed that day over and over and over again. If I would've been with them, I would've been driving, and I could've swerved in time, and everyone would be alive. God damn it!" He stomped his boot down, shaking the planks below him. "After I buried my girls, I felt like I was living a nightmare, Hell on earth. And, umm, I slipped deep into addiction, drugs and drinking, and around the one-year anniversary, I couldn't take the guilt no more, so I decided to come clean. I went to the sheriff and told him everything. Noah, the girls, and what I did. I was prepared for him to lock me up on the spot, but he just filed a report and told me he'd investigate it."

The man gazed past Hannah. She took a quick peek over her shoulder, half expecting an ambush. Nothing.

"Well, that very night, I had some visitors come to my house. They had a couple of baseball bats, and they beat me within inches of my life. And when they left, they told me to keep my mouth shut about my time in Echo Canyon or I'd never see another sunrise. Those bastards broke my leg in seven places, and I haven't been able to walk without a severe limp since."

"What did the sheriff say about your beating?" Hannah found a slight pleasure saying it.

"I never reported it to that bastard. He was the only person I told, so I'm certain he told Noah, and Noah dispatched some goons to break my legs. Fuck, I wouldn't be surprised if the sheriff was visiting Echo Canyon as well."

"Lovely."

"I said you wouldn't want to hear what I had to say."

"It's fine, please continue." Hannah said.

The man removed a plastic pint of Evan Williams from his jacket, took a deep swig, then offered it to Hannah. She stared at the bottle for a moment, calculating the odds of catching a virus or disease transmitted through saliva. But she grabbed the bottle and took a long pull off it regardless, choking as she swallowed.

"I was in the hospital for two weeks, and spent most of my time in the room where Julia had passed. It was like some kind of cruel fucking joke. Well, after I got out, I planned to leave this fucking town, but between the hospital bills and not being able to work because my leg is fucked, I was broke and stuck here forever."

He paused for what felt like ten seconds.

"Last year, I got diagnosed with lung cancer. It's pretty much spread everywhere. Brain, liver, my bones, you name it. I'm a walking tumor. I mean, a good day for me is one where I'm not constantly pissing blood."He half laughed, half coughed. "And I'm positive it's from my work in Echo Canyon. Everything in those buildings had lead paint and was covered in asbestos, and who knows what other cancer-causing shit."

He wiped away tears with the back of his sleeve.

"I know I'm on borrowed time, and in fact, I'm surprised I'm still here. Each time I close my eyes, I pray that I'll be reunited with my girls instead of spending an eternity next to that son of a bitch Noah."

Hannah realized this was a deathbed confession. One last plea to save his soul. Pointless, she thought. She wasn't a believer in heaven or hell, good or evil, but if the devil did exist, there was no saving this man. And she was fine with that.

"I'm still paying for what I did in Echo Canyon. Every single fucking day," he said.

Fear filled the man's eyes, and his face was turning

gray. He probably hadn't uttered the story in years, maybe decades, and now, knowing that he was near the end, he seemingly realized that there was no saving his soul.

At the halfway point between Red Mesa and Echo Canyon, Hannah pulled over to the shoulder, put the car in park, and drummed on the steering wheel. She watched the road in front of her. Five minutes. Ten minutes. Fifteen. Not a single car in either direction.

Hannah stabbed her cigarette into the ashtray, then pulled the trunk latch and got out and walked to the back of the car. She removed the spare tire, placed it on the highway, and rolled it down the embankment. The tire continued for about ten feet before falling over on its side among the sage brush and dirt.

Last night, after returning to the room, Hannah had poured a stiff drink and begun brainstorming a cover for why she was visiting Echo Canyon. Initially, she decided she'd tell locals she was doing some sightseeing of southern Utah. But the longer she thought about it, and the more she drank, the worse that plan sounded. A young female, traveling alone, and opting to stay in a remote town during off-season might raise some suspicions.

In the middle of her fourth whiskey, a better but still risky plan came to her. Car troubles. She would ditch the spare tire, then puncture one of her tires just outside of Echo Canyon and hobble into town on a rim.

From her time in small Colorado towns, Hannah knew nonessential businesses were usually closed on the weekends. And she was certain, in a town like Echo Canyon, almost everything would be. Her car would be stuck at the service station until at least Monday morning, and that would give her a valid excuse to be in town for a couple of days.

Even though she wasn't 100 percent sold on the new plan, it was better than strolling into town and pretending to be a tourist in the middle of December.

Moments after she slammed the trunk, a single-engine Cessna flew over. It was at a very low altitude, low enough she could almost make out the markings on the fuselage. The engine puttered for what felt like minutes, then the nose started to drop, and she thought she was going to witness a plane crash. The plane disappeared behind the canyon walls and she stood still, listening to the drone of the engine until it faded into nothing.

Back in the car, Hannah opened her wallet and took out her driver's license, credit cards, library card, and any other identification with the name "Hannah Jacobs." She placed them in a Ziploc baggie, then reached over the center console and stuffed the baggie deep into the back seat cushion. She was certain it was the best hiding spot in the Camry, and confident the baggie wouldn't be found. And if it was, that would mean they were already onto her ruse, and concealing her identity wouldn't matter anyway.

Glancing into the rearview mirror, Hannah watched the motionless horizon. This was the point of no return. Go back to St. George, get her 4Runner, and drive home to Denver, disregarding Steve and Margaret, or continue with her makeshift plan to find Emily.

"Fuck it," she said. Then she put the car in gear and merged back onto 289.

When Echo Canyon was in sight, Hannah pulled over, jumped out, and jammed a pocket knife between the treads of the rear driver's-side tire. She yanked out the knife, and the tire began to hiss.

For the first few miles, she couldn't tell a difference, but when she entered the city limits, the car started to wobble. By the time she reached the service station, the rim was grinding against the pavement, shooting sparks.

After grabbing her bag and locking the car, then checking and double-checking that the doors were indeed locked, Hannah started across the lot toward the highway.

Two blocks back was the Echo Canyon Motel, a single-story building with about twenty rooms that stretched in a long, straight line. When Hannah rolled by, there wasn't a single car in the parking lot, and if not for the flashing vacancy sign, it could've been mistaken as being permanently closed.

The town was something out of a movie, or a postcard. The road and sidewalk were pristine. No gravel, or dirt or twigs. No candy bar wrappers, not even a cigarette butt. Almost like any garbage was instantly put on a truck and hauled out of town.

She had an uneasy feeling that someone was watching her, maybe many someones, but when she looked around, she couldn't see anyone. She began to second-guess her decision, and cursed herself for crippling her only means of escape. Some of her best decisions originated from being inebriated, as well as some of her worst. This ranked up with the worst.

When she entered the motel lobby, a girl who couldn't have been older than sixteen stood erect behind the counter, as if she'd been expecting Hannah to walk in at that exact moment. Hannah flashed a smile, and the girl returned one.

"How can I help you?" the girl said.

"I was wondering if there's a mechanic, or someone

that could help me out. I got a flat somewhere on 289, and lucky me, I don't have a spare."

The girl tilted her head. "Oh my gosh, that is a bummer. And umm, I hate to be the bearer of bad news, but the garage is closed on the weekends. It doesn't open until Monday morning at eight."

Hannah shrugged. "Yeah, I saw the hours posted on the door. I guess that's going to put a wrench in my travel plans, I was hoping to make it to Zion today."

"Hmm, I don't know if any mechanics are open in Red Mesa, but maybe if they are, they could come down and fix it, or give you a tow back up there. Do you want to look through the phone book?"

"That sounds expensive."

The girl nodded. "I would reckon it's more than a room for a few nights here."

"I reckon so."

With a cheery demeanor, she said, "Well, the good news is the garage is owned by my cousin Joseph. He's an amazing mechanic, and can fix anything from a car to a tractor to a refrigerator, so you're in good hands. And after your car is fixed, if you decide you want to stay longer, we have plenty of vacancies."

Hannah glanced to the empty parking lot. "I'd say so. It looks like I'm the only person here."

"Yeah, it's somewhat uncommon to get guests this time of year, but on the plus side, that means you have the entire place to yourself," she said with a fixed smile.

"Lucky me," Hannah said. "Let's start off with two nights, and I'll add more if I change my mind."

The girl nodded silently, tapping buttons on the cash register. "If you wanna pay cash, you get a 5 percent discount, so with tax it'll be $47.98. Or if you wanna pay with a credit card or check, it'll be $50.50."

"For both nights?"

The girl nodded slowly.

"Let's do cash," Hannah said.

"Can I get an ID? We just need one in case there's any damages to the room during your stay."

Hannah nodded, then slid the license with her picture and the name "Tiffany Barnes" across the counter.

Without looking up from the paperwork, the girl said, "If you're hungry, the Echo Cafe is across the street, and it's delicious. I love the blueberry pancakes."

Hannah looked over her shoulder to the restaurant. "Are they still open?"

"Yeah, until three. And just a heads-up, us and them are the only places open in Echo Canyon on Saturdays, and on Sundays, everything is closed. So, unless you have an emergency, it might be hard to get a hold of anyone."

"Luckily I have a bag of chips so I won't starve tomorrow."

"I could drop you off a sandwich if you'd like."

"That'd be great," Hannah said.

The girl smiled again and slid a key across the counter. "We're doing some work in one and two, so you have room three. Oh, I don't think I mentioned it, but all the rooms are nonsmoking."

"You don't have to worry about that, I've never smoked a cigarette in my life," Hannah said as she walked out of the lobby.

In the room, Hannah turned on the bathroom fan, stood on the toilet lid, lit a cigarette, and blew cigarette smoke into the fan like a high school kid smoking a joint in their parents' downstairs bathroom. Halfway through the cigarette, she grew paranoid someone would smell the smoke, so she dropped it into the bowl, flushed the toilet, and watched as it disappeared down the drain.

As she walked to the diner, she saw a group of six teenagers sitting at a picnic bench—three girls on one side and three boys on the other.

The girls wore long-sleeved, ankle-length dresses and black flats, and not a single one had makeup on. Every girl wore her hair in the same style, tightly pulled back in a bun. The boys all wore white dress shirts, white ties, black trousers, and black loafers. They all had crew cuts and no facial hair.

Almost in unison, they all looked up at Hannah. She smiled and waved, but she only received a partial wave back from the girls. They stared for a bit longer, then looked away and started talking among themselves, sporadically looking back at her.

As Hannah got closer, they all got up and disappeared behind a building. She watched for a moment, waiting for them to return, but she didn't see them again.

When she turned back to the highway, she saw a woman and a young girl on a horse-drawn carriage. Neither of them made eye contact.

"What the fuck is going on here?" Hannah murmured.

The diner looked like it was built in the 1960s and probably hadn't been renovated since. Something off a movie set, with the waitress, the cook, and an elderly customer straight out of central casting. On the wall was a black-and-white photograph of a barn surrounded by a small shanty town with about a dozen structures. The caption read "Year One – 1956."

"Sit anywhere you like," the waitress said.

Hannah sat in the first booth. Within seconds, the waitress was at the table with a menu and a glass of water. She didn't look a day over sixteen either, and she and the girl from the motel looked and acted almost identical. Maybe sisters, or first cousins.

"Are you and the girl at the motel related?"

She giggled. "Yeah. That's Amber, she's my cousin."

"I see the resemblance."

The girl smiled. "What brings you to our lovely town?" she said, twirling her hair. Her eyes were warm and trusting, but that could be a trap. Again, Hannah reminded herself to be extremely cautious with everyone, even innocent-looking teenage girls. "We normally don't see many tourists this time of year."

"I wouldn't call myself a tourist, more of a passerby. All I wanted was to take the scenic route down 289, and my stupid car got a flat. And it sounds like the shop doesn't open until Monday, so I'm stuck here until then."

"I'm sorry to hear that, love, that's no fun. Luckily Joseph, the head mechanic, is amazing, and I'm sure he'll have your car fixed in no time," she said, as if she were reading from a script.

"That's what I've heard. Just curious, what kind of tourists do you guys get around here?"

"Oh, mostly hikers doing Wolf Buttes. It's about twenty miles east of town," the waitress said, pointing out the window. "It's a big hiking destination, but the road is only open from May until October."

"Hence the lack of people."

The waitress nodded. "When it's open, we're busy, and when it's closed, it's dead like this." She stared at Hannah for a moment. "I don't mean to rush you, but do you know what you're having, sweetie? I think the cook wants to start closing up so he can get out of here."

After skimming the menu, Hannah pointed to a picture and glanced up. "Give me the lumberjack. Scrambled, bacon, and Amber recommended the blueberry pancakes."

The girl rolled her eyes. "Of course she did. She eats

them like four times a week. She eats them so much she's going to turn into a darn blueberry."

"And can I get a coffee?"

"Umm, I'm sorry, but we don't serve coffee. As a matter of fact, we don't serve anything with caffeine, but we have milk, iced tea, lemonade, and a bunch of different flavors of tea. I can bring you out the box so you can see what we have."

"Milk is fine," Hannah said.

The girl started to turn, then stopped. "And if you need anything, just give a holler. I'm Ashley."

Hannah had been about to ask her name, hoping that by some dumb chance she was Anna. Nope, no such luck.

Hannah smiled. "I'm Tiffany."

"That's a lovely name."

About ten minutes later, the waitress set the food on the table, Hannah stared at the plate, fork in hand, contemplating if the food was drugged. Maybe some type of sedative. Leaning into the booth, she peered into the kitchen and studied the cook. Nothing out of the ordinary. She decided the odds were slim, and she was starving, so she decided to take her chances.

Moments after Hannah finished eating, Ashley sat down across from her. "I'm such a ding-dong, but since you're going to be in town, you have to come to our dance tonight."

"Dance?" Hannah repeated.

"Yes, there's a dance every month, but the one tonight is the Winter Dance. It's the biggest one of the year. You have to go!"

"I don't know," Hannah said.

Ashley turned her head sideways and raised her eyebrows. "Come on, what else are you going to do? Everything is going to be closed, and like half the town is going to be there. It's going to be so much fun." She leaned forward. "I'm not going to take no for an answer."

Hannah looked out the window and watched another horse-drawn carriage trot by.

"I really don't have anything to wear to a dance."

Ashely inspected Hannah. "I think you might be in luck, because I happen to have a couple dresses that I think would fit you perfect."

"Oh no, I wouldn't want to trouble you."

"It's no trouble at all." She pointed across the street. "See those apartments, I live in the bottom one in the middle. It makes the commute super easy."

Hannah reluctantly nodded. "Okay, let me see what you have."

"Awesome! Wait here, I'll be back in a jiffy."

Ten minutes later, Ashley returned with two dresses and draped them over the booth across from Hannah.

"What one do you like?"

The dresses looked identical. "They're both nice, but I think I like the one on the left more," Hannah said, faking a smile.

"Perfect, go in the bathroom and try it on."

As Hannah walked to the dance, a blood-orange sun sank behind the building, and she said a silent prayer that she'd see the sunrise the following morning. She was 90 percent certain that no one knew her true identity; it was that 10 percent that terrified her.

Before she left, Hannah looked in the mirror and barely recognized herself. The dress covered almost her entire body, all but her face, hands, and ankles. She might as well have been wrapped in a blanket. The dress, combined with no makeup and her hair being pulled straight back, made her look like a carbon copy of every girl in town.

The moment Hannah walked into the gymnasium, something in the air felt different, sinister. A pit formed deep in her stomach, like she didn't belong here. For a second, she considered turning around and going back to her room, but she'd already been seen, and leaving now would only raise suspicion.

There were probably a few hundred people inside the gymnasium. Some on the dance floor, some getting refreshments, but the majority were sitting at tables. Wallflowers watching the dancers.

Everyone was Caucasian, most with brown or blond hair. No one overweight, no one had a tattoo or a piercing. Not a single one. The men and women were all wearing the exact same clothing as the teenagers at the picnic bench, down to the color of their shoes and ties. If someone had told Hannah it was a huge family reunion, she would've believed it. They all looked like they were made at the same factory from two molds, one male and one female.

She wondered if some were the product of inbreeding. While researching, she came across a report about a rare birth defect that causes brain malformation, slow development, seizures and unusual facial features. There had only been about a dozen cases worldwide until the last decade, when a cluster of over thirty exploded in Echo Canyon.

Seven Day Saints claim it is due to heavy metals in the drinking water, but medical experts who refer to it as Echo Syndrome, say the true cause can be attributed to parents who were first cousins.

The playlist consisted of soft rock bands—REO Speedwagon, Chicago, Michael McDonald, and Steely Dan. Music suitable for a grocery store, like they found a

"Best Of" cassette in a gas station bargain bin. She hated soft rock more than she hated country, and had a theory that people who enjoyed it had lower IQs.

Hannah had a weird feeling that everyone was staring at her, but every time she looked at someone, they turned away, almost like they were purposely avoiding her gaze. It felt like she was in a horror movie, and at any moment, a bucket of pig's blood was going to be dumped on her head.

A small girl, maybe ten, appeared from the crowd and offered Hannah a plastic cup of what appeared to be punch. Before she drank, Hannah inspected it. Nothing seemed suspicious.

She smiled and thanked the girl, then took a sip, swishing it in her mouth for a second before swallowing. As Hannah watched the girl walk away, someone came from behind and tapped her on the shoulder.

"You made it!" Ashley yelled.

"I sure did," she said, faking another smile.

"Come on, I want you to meet everyone."

Ashely grabbed Hannah's hand and started introducing her to about half of the people in the gymnasium. "This is my brother," "This is my best friend," "This is my cousin," "This is my other cousin," "And my third cousin," "This is Amber, but you already met her.'"

After thirty minutes of "Nice to meet you" and retelling the story of why she was in town, Hannah told Ashley she was going to sit down and rest her feet for a few minutes.

"Of course. Get some rest, and when you're ready, come find me. We're going to dance the night away."

Hannah retreated to the bleachers, climbing to the second-to-last row. It was the best vantage point in the entire gymnasium. Over and over and over, she skimmed the crowd. People danced and people ate, people came and people left, but there was no sight of Emily.

Maybe she was sick and had decided to stay home. Maybe she'd quit Seven Day Saints and already left Echo Canyon. Maybe she was being held captive. Or maybe she was dead.

After twenty minutes, Hannah climbed down the bleachers, found Ashley, and asked for directions to the bathroom.

"It's back past that door, about halfway down on your right. You can't miss it," Ashley said.

When Hannah pushed open the bathroom door, a girl was washing her hands at a sink. The recognition was immediate.

"Emily?" Hannah said.

The girl studied her in the mirror. For a moment, she remained completely still, and a chill ran down Hannah's spine. Something inside of her screamed, *Run. Run.* Go back to the motel, grab her bag, get out of town, and never come back.

The girl turned off the water, then slowly turned around. "Oh my gosh, Hannah, is that you?" she said, rubbing her eyes. "Hannah, it is you!"

Hannah nodded and whispered, "Yes. It's me"

Emily ran toward her and wrapped her arms around her. "I can't believe it's really you. Please tell me this isn't a dream."

After a quick embrace, Hannah took a step back. "Why aren't you at the dance?"

"I'm working in the kitchen. Someone has to make food for all of these people. The more important question is, what are you doing here?"

"I came to see if you're okay."

With a confused look, Emily said, "Well, why wouldn't I be?"

The bathroom door flew open, and both their heads

turned. The same girl who'd given Hannah the punch walked in, smiled, then disappeared into a stall. For a moment, Hannah thought the girl was following her, but she decided it had to be a coincidence.

"Can we go somewhere a little more private to talk?" Hannah whispered, eyeing the bathroom door.

"Is everything okay?" Emily said.

With eyes wide, Hannah tapped her finger against her lips and whispered, "Yes, I just need to talk to you in private."

"Okay, okay. We can go out back. There shouldn't be anyone out there," Emily whispered, gesturing to the door.

She wrapped her fingers around Hannah's wrist and led her through a series of hallways. Left, right, right, right, left. Past office doors, a storage room, the kitchen, and a door leading to a flight of stairs.

At the end of the hallway was a set of double doors, Emily pressed on the bar and pushed the metal doors open. They stepped outside and the doors crashed behind them, cutting off the music from the dance.

The night was bitter, but Hannah barely noticed, her unease temporarily shielding her from the cold.

Again, Emily wrapped her arms around Hannah. After twenty seconds, she took a step back and looked her up and down. "You're the last person I thought I'd see here. I've missed you so much!"

Hannah placed her hand on Emily's shoulder.

"Your father hired me to find you. He said he hasn't talked to you in almost two years. He is very concerned, and if I'm being honest, I'm a little worried myself."

"Always the worrier. He was like this when I went away to tennis camp," Emily said, rolling her eyes. "He knows I'm okay."

"No, he doesn't, and this isn't tennis camp. Why haven't you called him?"

Emily shrugged. "I don't know. I've been busy around here. I guess time just slipped away from me."

"That's an excuse for two weeks, or maybe two months, but not two years."

Emily looked past Hannah for a few seconds, then returned her gaze. "I can promise you I'm fine."

Hannah stared at her, attempting to gauge if she was lying. The voice inside her began chanting again, this time louder. *Run, run, run.*

"If you're fine, why have you completely cut off communication from him and Margaret?"

"They don't understand my life here. My purpose, my calling. I tried to tell them, but they didn't want to listen. They're blind to everything that is happening in the world," Emily said, with a hint of aggression.

"And what do you believe is happening?"

Emily half smiled. "I'm not at liberty to speak about that, but I could introduce you to Kenneth, and he can tell you everything you need to know. I promise, if you spend ten minutes with him, you will be changed forever."

"I don't need my life changed."

As if typing a message in morse code, Emily began frantically tapping on her thigh. "I just want you to see what I've seen."

Hannah thought about how to respond. She wanted to shake her stepsister by the shoulders and scream that she was part of a cult, but Hannah knew that would only alienate Emily and put Hannah herself in even more peril. She decided the safest plan was to pretend like she was interested in a meeting.

"How about a trade-off? I'll meet with Kenneth if you come back to my room and call your father first."

"Okay, I just have to get approval from Kenneth before I make the call."

"And what if you don't ask permission?"

Emily frowned as if she'd taken a bite out of a lemon. "I don't understand. Why would I not ask him?"

Paranoid that someone might be listening, Hannah lowered her voice. "I don't think it's safe to talk about this right here."

Emily cocked her head, and confusion came over her face, like Hannah was speaking a foreign language. She looked away for a moment, and when she came back, it was like she was looking right through Hannah.

"You're not making any sense," Emily said.

"I've heard stories about Kenneth and Seven Day Saints. Some very disturbing stuff."

"Like what?"

"I'm not going to talk about it out here."

Emily's eyes darted to the field behind them, avoiding contact. That worried Hannah enough for her to take a step back.

To the south, a train thundered over the tracks. It could've been two miles away or twenty. Either way, too far for an escape.

"What do you want me to do to prove that I'm okay?"

"Again, come back to my room and call your father," Hannah said through clenched teeth.

"Fine, whatever. I think you guys are freaking out about nothing, though."

"Okay. Right now? And you're not going to ask Kenneth or anyone else for approval?"

"Yes, yes, geez, what else do I need to say!" Emily shouted.

"Please, keep your voice down," Hannah said, gesturing downward with her palms.

But at that moment, her heart sank. She realized it was a trap, a setup. Everything was too easy. Strolling into town, getting invited to the dance, finding Emily in mere hours, and being able to sneak away from everyone. She was prey, about to be surrounded by a ravenous pack of wolves.

"Come on, let's go," Emily said, extending her hand.

Hannah nodded and took a deep breath. Just as she was about to turn and run, she saw something out of the corner of her eye. Before she could react, the light left her.

SIX

When Hannah came to, she took several deep breaths, then lifted her head and began to open her eyes, but it was all blurry. The ringing in her skull felt worse than any hangover she could remember, and she instantly lowered her head and closed her eyes, shielding them from the light.

She was groggy, and her memory was disjointed. *Where the fuck am I?* She started to attempt to piece back together her last memories, but everything felt fuzzy, like a dream.

Slowly, it came back to her. She was in Echo Canyon, at the dance with Emily, and then what? That was where everything went dark.

Finally, after a minute, maybe two, she opened her eyes again. In the corner, a man stood erect, donned in all white. White shoes, white slacks, and a white dress shirt.

Suffering from double vision, she could barely make out his features, and if she had to pick him out of a police lineup, all she'd be able to say was that he was tall and white. He remained completely still, and for a moment Hannah thought he was a mannequin, but then he turned and started to the door.

"Wait, wait! Where the fuck am I?" she croaked.

The man disappeared, locking the door behind him.

Hannah raised her hand to flip him off, and for the first time felt the handcuff around her left wrist. The cuff was attached to a long, metal chain that dropped to the floor and snaked a few feet before disappearing into a dark doorway.

Hannah held the chain up and pulled. It went taut, clanking against something that sounded like a pipe. Maybe plumbing for a sink or toilet. Without even trying, she knew it was futile to reach the door.

"Fuck," she muttered, shaking her head.

She had no idea how long she'd been out, and she didn't even want to guess. What she did know was the splitting headache continued to get worse. Reaching back, she felt the bump, half the size of a tennis ball. It hurt to the touch.

When she lifted the bedsheet, a faint smell of urine entered the air. With her free hand, she felt the mattress beneath her. Everything was dry. She wasn't sure how long it took urine to completely dry, but it must've been more than a few hours.

Minus her shoes, she wore the same clothes from the dance, seemingly undisturbed. She stared for a moment, then let go of the sheet and slid to the edge of the bed.

The room was probably twelve-by-twelve, and concrete from floor to ceiling. The door the man had exited through was in the opposite corner, as far away from the bed as possible, and looked more like a walk-in cooler door than something in a house.

The walls, ceiling, and floor were painted white, except

for one spot on the wall, directly across from the bed. There, written in two-foot letters, were the words "Love Thy Brother and Sister." And even though her vision was still a little blurry, she could read it as clear as day.

When Hannah was twelve, she'd had a gap between her front teeth that she could slip her pinky through. Most of the girls in her class made fun of her, but one of them, Becky, was particularly harsh. Over the course of the year, the bullying from Becky got worse—tripping, pushing, and spitting. Then, one day, she grabbed Hannah by the shoulders and yanked her down into a pile of dog shit. When Hannah looked up, it felt like the entire school was watching and laughing at her. Hannah ran home, locked herself in her room, and cried the entire night.

Casey had had enough, and after Hannah told her what happened and who did it, Casey waited for Becky in the bathroom. Once alone with her, Casey threw the girl to the ground, and with a foot on her neck, told her if she ever touched Hannah again, Casey, along with some of her friends would find her after school and make her eat dog shit until she threw up.

Becky never bullied Hannah again. Hell, she didn't even say more than a few words to her for the rest of the year.

All Hannah wanted was for Casey to kick in the door and save her again. But Casey was dead, and if someone didn't come to her rescue, Hannah herself would probably not be long for this world.

Just as she was about to explore the room where the chain disappeared into, the door crept open and Emily stepped in, closing it softly behind her.

"I thought you'd be awake a while ago, but nope, you were really out."

She sauntered to the bed, then rested both palms on the mattress. Maybe it had been Hannah's initial excitement at finding Emily, or maybe it was the bathroom lighting in the gymnasium, but looking directly into her eyes now, Hannah could see they were soulless, dead inside. If she'd seen those eyes the night of the dance, she would've turned and run.

"How is your head feeling? Hopefully not that bad."

She raised her hand toward Hannah's head, but Hannah slapped it away. Emily held her hand up for a moment, then placed it back down.

"I'm so sorry we had to knock you out, but it was for your safety as much as mine and everyone else's."

Hannah wanted to leap out of bed and wrap her hands around Emily's neck, but she knew with one hand chained, the attempt would be useless.

"We weren't sure if you had a firearm or not. I figured you wouldn't, but better safe than sorry."

Emily waited for Hannah to say something, but Hannah remained still, lips pursed, breathing steadily through her nose.

"Silent treatment, huh? I get it, I'm sure you're a little upset that we had to bring you here, but I promise in a few months, you'll be grateful that we did."

Hannah didn't budge, trying her best to ignore Emily's presence.

Reaching into her pocket, Emily removed Hannah's fake ID and held it in between her thumb and index finger, casually flicking it.

"Tiffany Barnes, huh? That is a cute name. I like it. I mean, it didn't really work though, because within like twenty minutes, I was informed you might be in town. I dropped everything and hurried down to the diner to see with my own eyes, and I couldn't believe it was you, because I thought you're smarter than that." Emily shrugged and gave an uneven smile. "I'm curious, how did you see this playing out? You find me and convince me to leave, and we skip out of here hand in hand?"

Hannah remained silent and still.

"My gosh, where are my manners, you must be thirsty. Can I get you something to drink? Water? Milk? An apple juice?"

"I don't need anything from you, or Kenneth, or anyone else." Hannah stopped herself before she said something she'd regret.

"Aww, I finally get a response," Emily said, grinning. "Look around, Hannah. If you want your time here to be easy, you'll need to learn how to play nice."

As much as Hannah hated to admit it, Emily was right. At that moment, they dictated the rules. Even if she could slip out of the handcuff and somehow open the door, she had no clue what lay beyond it.

Patience was never a strong trait of hers, but if she wanted to survive, she'd have to exercise it and wait for the perfect opportunity. *Don't get impulsive. Don't do anything stupid. Repeat, don't do anything stupid.*

"No, I don't need anything right now," Hannah said, fighting the urge to scream.

Emily stared back, then strolled to a chair by the door and dragged it across the floor to the bed. She sat with her elbows on her knees.

"Who do you think dictates what happens to you in here?"

Reluctantly, Hannah said, "You and Kenneth."

"And who do you think dictates when you eat, and what you eat?"

"You and Kenneth."

"And who do you think allows you access to that bathroom? Making it so you don't have to wear a diaper."

Hannah turned away. "You," she said. Her voice was dry.

Emily smiled. "We've never had anyone expire down here, and I really don't want it to start with you." She traced the flower pattern on the bed sheet with her index finger. "Can I ask a question? I mean, I'm going to ask it no matter what, but I guess what I'm asking is, will you answer it?"

"Sure," Hannah said.

"Are you getting help from anyone? I bet you are, and I'd bet everything it was that Indian with the messed-up face. Roger. Right, it had to be him. I don't know who else would've."

"I don't know who you're talking about."

In her head, she could hear Roger's voice warning her, begging her not to go to Echo Canyon. If only she had listened to him.

"I think you know who I'm talking about. I mean, I can see it written all over your face."

"I don't know anyone named Roger."

"I really thought after what happened to his dog, he would leave us alone, but I guess not. Maybe it's time to pay him another visit."

As Hannah bit down on the inside of her lip, she was certain her teeth were about to tear straight through flesh.

"Actually, would you happen to know if he got another dog?" Emily said.

"Please leave him alone. I talked to him for like ten minutes maybe, not even that. He didn't want to help, and he warned me to stay away. The only thing we talked about was his dog passing, I promise."

Emily gave her a long look. "I don't believe you, but we'll have plenty of time to talk about Roger later." She grabbed Hannah's hand and squeezed it. "I'm really happy that you came here, Hannah. I really am."

Hannah glared for a moment, then turned away. Her stomach growled. It felt like it was twisting and pulling in every direction. Between her head and her stomach, she was having a hard time concentrating.

Emily shifted in the chair, and it let out a haunting squeal. For a moment, Hannah thought it was going to buckle under her.

"It is so nice to see your face after all these years. Do you remember when you came up for Thanksgiving and we played Uno all night long?"

"Yeah, and I let you win."

Emily smiled. "Did you know after you left, I begged and begged my dad and Margaret to see you again, but they both said no, that you'd be a bad influence on me." She twirled her hair gingerly. "Well, a few months later, I found your phone number and address in Margaret's desk. I called a few times, but you didn't answer, so I waited until everyone was out of the house. Then I snuck out, and walked down to a bus stop. I didn't know what I was expecting to happen—I guess I thought I was going to show up on your doorstep and we'd hang out and play games, watch movies and eat junk food. Pretty dumb, huh?"

The story reminded Hannah of when she took a shuttle to Stapleton Airport after Casey's death, with no true destination.

"Well, five minutes before the bus got there, my dad rolls up and tells me to get in the car. I don't think I've ever seen him that mad before or since. Besides school, he barely let me out of my room for months. I couldn't believe I was being punished for trying to see my sister."

That night, when Emily came to her room so many years ago, it was an attempt to form a sisterly relationship. If Hannah hadn't ignored it, maybe neither of them would be in Echo Canyon right now.

"I've never told anyone this before, but I got a B minus in AP calculus when I was a sophomore, and my dad was so pissed because it was going to lower my 4.0 GPA. When he found out, he shoved me so hard that I broke my wrist," Emily said, admiring her right wrist. "But you know what? It worked. I never got anything lower than an A again. I mean, I had to give one of my teachers a blowjob for an A, but I'd trade that any day over another broken bone."

Hannah wasn't sure if Emily was telling the truth or trying to portray herself as the victim and Margaret and Steve as the villains.

Emily cleared her throat. "Can I tell you something else? Yeah?" She didn't wait for a response. "Okay, I never liked Margaret. I actually hate her. I actually hate my dad too. Maybe more than Margaret, and that is the reason I left."

Hannah didn't respond.

"Do you love Margaret? Or even like her?"

Silence.

"Your lack of an answer is all I need. I'm glad we're on the same page. I always thought she was a gold-digger, and I wish my dad never married her, but I get it. After my mom died, he was lonely, and she filled that void. I don't know if he loves her, but he's scared of being alone, and some people would rather be miserable than alone. He probably was going to marry the first woman that showed interest in him. Probably the first woman that got him off."

Emily paused for a second, then continued. "Didn't she just leave you and your dad after Casey got murdered? That is pretty fucked up, if you ask me. I still can't fathom why you agree to help her and my dad."

Hannah remained silent. As much as she hated to admit it, Emily was right.

"They played you like a fiddle. Hook, line and sinker. I wish I could've been a fly on the wall when they gave you the sob story about how their precious daughter was abducted by a 'brainwashing cult,'" Emily said, making air quotes with her fingers. "They don't care about you. They don't care about anyone except themselves. And when they figure out you're not coming back, they'll just hire someone else like they did with Roger, and the guy before him, and the guy before him." Emily rose from the chair and dragged it back to the wall. "I mean, I'm glad you did take the job, though, because that brought you here, to me. And if everything goes to plan, you'll always be here."

"That's the plan, keeping me locked up in this town forever?" Hannah said, her voice almost going up an octave.

"Shh. No need to get angry." Emily brought her index finger to her mouth, kissing it for a fleeting moment. "I can promise, once you meet Kenneth, you're never going to want to leave."

"You really think that?"

"I know it," Emily said.

Hannah stared at her, saying nothing, trying not to blink. She tried to think of a clever comeback, but thoughts were scattered, and the headache was becoming worse. With each breath, her head pounded, feeling like it was going to explode.

As much as it pained her to ask, she said, "Can I please get an aspirin?"

"Oh no, sweetie, that poison is strictly forbidden here." She chuckled. "No aspirin, no Advil, no prescription pills. Nothing of the sort. As well as no alcohol, cigarettes, caffeine. We live a clean life here, no vices of any kind."

"I guess I should be lucky I'm not a diabetic."

"I'll bring you some tea. That should help. Oh yeah, and one more thing."

Emily started to the door, and Hannah followed her with her eyes until she disappeared. Moments later she returned, holding a perfectly folded bedsheet.

"It smells like you might've wet the bed while you were out, so here's a clean sheet, and you'll find a clean change of clothes in the bathroom." Emily pointed to the doorway where the chain disappeared. "Just leave the dirty stuff on the floor. And this room doesn't have great heating, so it might get cold at night. If you do get cold, there are a couple quilts under the bed."

Emily stared at Hannah, waiting for her to say something.

"Thank you," Hannah finally said. She didn't want to say it, but she felt Emily wasn't going to budge until she did. Hannah knew she would have to concede on some things she was opposed too, like saying "please" and "thank you," or else her time alive here might be short.

"You're welcome, Hannah. Now get some rest, because Kenneth is going to be here later tonight. And a word of wisdom, when he enters the room, sit up and give a nice, big smile. He likes that, and it'll get you guys off on the right foot."

"I can't wait to meet him," she said, faking a smile.

Emily tapped her chin. "Let's see, what else? If you need to tinkle, the bathroom is in there. I'll get someone to bring you dinner in a few. And I feel like I shouldn't have to say this, but don't try to do anything stupid. There's a guard outside your door, twenty-four hours a day."

"I wouldn't think of it."

"Good." Emily blew a kiss. "Toodles, sis. See you real soon."

Just as Hannah was starting to doze off, the door opened and a man entered the room. From the pictures she'd seen of Kenneth Pratt, she was certain this was him, but it looked like he'd aged decades. Almost like a completely different person.

For some reason, Hannah expected Kenneth to be some larger-than-life figure, but he was probably five-foot-five, with a beer belly and a very bad comb-over. If she saw him on the street, she'd think he was some schlubby, divorced accountant who owned a CPA firm that barely stayed afloat.

His eyes were glassy, his face bloated, and beads of sweat dotted his forehead, glistening in the light. Hannah had seen the look countless times in cocaine addicts, and she was certain he was on something.

He closed the door and leaned back into it, one palm flat on the metal, a smile from ear to ear. Hannah gave a quick, fake smile of her own, then averted her eyes.

"It's nice to finally meet you. Sorry it took so long, but my work in town is never done. Never ever," he said. When he stopped speaking, the smile returned to his face, like he required it in order to breathe.

Hannah gave a slight nod.

"How do you like your accommodations?" he said.

"It's fine."

After Emily left, Hannah had investigated the room. There was the bed, plus two weathered, wooden chairs that were out of Hannah's reach, and the two quilts under the bed as promised. One thing that Emily hadn't mentioned was that the metal bed frame was bolted to the floor. It wasn't going anywhere.

The bathroom was only a toilet and a small vanity

sink. There was a toothbrush and a half-used tube of toothpaste, one roll of toilet paper on top of the tank, and a dirty washcloth draped over the faucet. And no matter how long she let the water run, it never got hot.

"I am very fond of your sister. She is a great asset to me, and a valuable member to this community."

"She is not my sister," Hannah blurted out.

"Well, not by blood, so technically you are correct, but I doubt you would've come here if there wasn't some sort of bond between the two of you." He paused, waiting for Hannah to respond, but she remained still, her jaw locked. He smiled and pushed off the door.

"Your other sister—Casey, was it? I'm so sorry about her passing," he said warmly. "It must've been very difficult on you, especially at such a young age. I'm sure it still haunts you to this very day."

"Don't ever say her name again," Hannah said, trying to contain her anger.

Kenneth nodded as if to acknowledge her request. "What do you think of Echo Canyon?"

Hannah murmured something like "It's fine" again, unsure of the exact words.

"When my dad first stepped foot here, there was nothing, just the highway and tumbleweeds. The first few years were rough, and they lost some people, but he held strong, and it began to grow, then double and triple. Today, it's as big as it's ever been, and it's not going to stop. In less than ten years, I project we will be almost ten thousand strong. It's going to be something special. People are going to flock here from all over Utah, and from all over the world."

Kenneth was charismatic, and Hannah could see how a simple-minded person could fall under his spell, do his bidding. Hearing him speak, she understood the followers of Jonestown and the Branch Davidians, and the people of Echo Canyon.

"And Hannah, you can be part of that."

"I'll die before I'm part of this fucking place," she whispered under her breath.

Meticulously he walked about the room, then ran his index finger across "Love Thy Brother and Sister," as if each letter conjured special memories.

"I know I can help you."

"Yeah? You wanna help? How about you remove this handcuff and let me out of this room?" Hannah said, holding up her hand.

His smile grew. "I can't do that right now, but if you're a good girl, I'll consider some special accommodations."

Hannah glared at him, her lips tight.

He winked and continued. "Emily tells me you are a very talented private investigator, and that you, and you alone, solved the murder of your sister when the police couldn't. After hearing all that praise, I was very surprised when you strolled into town, and accepted the invitation to the dance, then blindly followed Emily to me, like a little mouse chasing cheese in a trap."

Kenneth walked toward the bed and hovered over her. His breath was vile—a mouth full of rotting teeth probably combined with gingivitis or periodontitis.

He began caressing her hair. She shut her eyes and tried to pretend it wasn't happening, to put her thoughts anywhere but this room, but it was to no avail. Each time she felt his warm breath, it pulled her right back.

"I've never felt hair so soft."

"Stop! Get your hands off of me!" Hannah screamed, no longer able to contain her rage. She'd known it'd only be a matter of time before she lost her cool, but she hadn't thought it'd be this fast.

Kenneth clutched a handful of hair and yanked her toward him. He leaned in, mere inches from her lips. He inhaled her scent, and just as she thought he was going to slam her head against the bed frame, he released her and walked away.

"What does that mean to you?" he said, pointing to the writing on the wall.

"I don't know, and I don't care."

He turned up his fingers, staring at his nails like he was going to bite them. Then he turned back to Hannah and continued strolling around the room.

"One night, my father was alone in a corn field in Kansas, and a spirit visited him, and told him to write down those very words. He said to go west, and find the promised land. The spirit wouldn't tell him what it all meant, but said it would be the start of a revolution." Kenneth smiled. "Without those five simple words, this community would cease to exist. It's the foundation of Echo Canyon, and what makes us one big, happy family."

"And what if someone in your family wants to leave?" Hannah said, then continued, not letting Kenneth answer. "You don't let them, do you? You lock them up in this room until they comply. Isn't that right?"

"It's for your own protection."

Hannah could see in his eyes that he'd never allow her to leave Echo Canyon. Even if she pretended like a devout follower, he was smarter than that. Nope, it'd be too risky, because if she ever told anyone about this place, everything he had, everything him and his father worked for, would be over.

"I don't need your fucking protection!"

"Yes, you do. There is—" He stopped and took a long, deep breath, then closed his eyes and exhaled. "There is a war going on out there right now, good versus evil."

"And you think you're the good guys? You think you're some sort of prophet who's going to protect everyone from evil?"

"I do. Outside of Echo Canyon, there is so much death and destruction. Addicts who will slice your throat for twenty dollars to get their next fix. Or a kid who walks into his classroom with an AK-47. Or someone who takes a bomb on a plane to kill hundreds! Do you think that is a healthy society? Do you think that's how people should live? In fear for their lives?"

"At least I have a choice. People here don't. I'd rather live free and die than ever follow a single command from you!"

"They follow what I say because it brings peace. In the history of Echo Canyon, there has never been a homicide, or a drug overdose, or a robbery, or a carjacking. Nothing of the sort. Not in over forty years."

Hannah laughed.

"You find that funny?" Kenneth said.

"I do, because I'm certain you've killed people. If not by your own hands, you've ordered one of your cronies to do it."

His smile grew. "You are so, so misguided, Hannah. The outside world has wanted to destroy what we've had for decades, and you fell into their trap, just like many others before you. They fear what we've built here."

"And what is that?"

"A utopia."

"It's a fucking cult, and just like David Koresh and Jim Jones, your day will come."

"You are wrong. So very wrong. There is a judgment date looming. Mass floods, mass drought, starvation, financial collapse, war among countries and neighbors. Your world will implode, and when it does, I guarantee you the masses will be begging to be a part of this community."

"Do you really believe all this bullshit you're spewing, or are you actually insane?"

Kenneth took a while to answer. "I promise, soon you'll understand, and when you do, you'll never want to leave again," he said, drawing the words out. "Just remember, the longer you deny it, the harder your time in this room will be."

She snorted. "Guess what, you piece of shit? I'll never believe anything you say."

"I mean you no harm, Hannah, but I can see you're lost, and I'm going to make it my personal mission to save you."

"Your words are meaningless! You're not going to be able to brainwash me like your followers who believe everything you utter." Hannah took a deep breath. "I can see right through you! I know exactly what you are."

"And what do you think that is?"

"A rapist and a pedophile. You groom girls before they're even teenagers and then force them into marriage, you sick fuck."

With calculated steps, he backed away and took a long look at Hannah, like he was appalled by the accusation, and had never heard it before.

"I've never raped a woman in my life. Quite the contrary. Every single one has offered themselves to me. They know it is their duty to bear my children, so this community will thrive forever with my bloodline."

And there it was, his justification for rape.

"Just like someday, you will ask me to lay with you," Kenneth said evenly.

"I will die before I touch you, you limp-dick fuck." The moment the words came out of her mouth, she regretted saying them. She knew calling him a rapist and pedophile wouldn't bother him because he didn't believe he was doing anything wrong, but questioning his manhood, that was the point of no return.

For the first time since Kenneth entered the room, fury entered his eyes. "Since you are new here, I've let it slide a few times, but profanity is not allowed in Echo Canyon. You will learn that in due time. Just like you will learn everything else that comes with being a member of this community."

Hannah screamed "fuck" at least ten times, until she was out of breath, and just as he was about to respond, she screamed it three more times.

"I can see you're going to be difficult."

"I haven't even started yet," Hannah said.

"Take a second and look around. Do you know where you are?" Kenneth gestured to the walls. "What this room is?"

"I don't know, your torture room?"

Kenneth turned his attention to a spider crawling on the wall. He walked toward it and leaned in, coming within inches. For a moment, Hannah thought he was going to inhale it. The room was silent as he watched the spider and Hannah watched him. Then he slammed his palm against the wall, crushing the spider. He kept his hand there for nearly ten seconds before slowly peeling it off. He admired his work, then wiped the remains onto his pants.

"You're in the basement, surrounded by six inches of solid concrete on every wall. This room was built back in the '60s as a fallout shelter to withstand a nuclear blast. When that door is closed, you could scream until your lungs bled, and no one would hear you."

Kenneth tilted his head back and screamed, the pitch piercing Hannah's eardrum. When he was finished, he turned back to Hannah and hit the wall with a closed fist.

"Now you try it."

Hannah remained still. Her hand trembled, and she tried to stifle it, but couldn't.

Without saying a word, Kenneth exited the room, then returned moments later, holding a branding iron and a propane torch. On the base of the iron were the letters "SDS." Hannah recognized it as the same design that was scarred on Roxy's thigh.

Two men dressed in white followed him in and stood on either side of the bed. Kenneth exchanged a few words with them, then turned back to Hannah.

Hannah glared at one, then the other, then back at Kenneth. She knew what was about to happen, and there was nothing she could do to stop it.

"Do you know what this is for?" he said, spinning the iron in his palm.

"Yeah, and you can go fuck yourself."

Hannah spat in his face. He tried to dodge it, but he was too slow, too late. He smiled and wiped the saliva with the back of his sleeve.

"You should not have done that, Hannah," he said, shaking his head.

Kenneth leaned the iron against the bed frame, then removed a lighter from his pocket and lit the torch. Both men stared down on her, expressionless, while Kenneth admired the flame. Methodically, he turned his gaze to Hannah.

"This can get up to a thousand degrees within sixty seconds," he said.

"You can't scare me, you fucking psychopath."

"Lift up her dress," Kenneth said, instructing the men, never taking his eyes off Hannah.

She briefly contemplated fighting them, but it would only prolong the inevitable. Hannah rolled her head to the side and shut her eyes. Seconds later, someone ripped off the quilt, and then almost simultaneously, two hands clutched her ankles and her dress was pulled up.

The room became still. The only sound Hannah could hear was the torch hissing.

"I was going to say this is going to hurt a little, but from the looks of it, you might actually enjoy this."

Her legs were forcefully separated. Someone knelt on the unchained hand and grabbed her chin, turning her head forward.

"Open your eyes," Kenneth said.

"Fuck off and die!"

"I promise you'll want to see this moment," he said. "Open your eyes! Open them! Stay with me, Hannah. Don't you dare try to escape this room!"

Everything became still again, and then Kenneth whispered in her ear, "This is the last time I'll say it. Open your eyes, or I'll cauterize your eyelids and you'll never see anything again."

Just as she began to open them, one of the men brought the back of his hand down onto her face. She let out a sharp groan as her entire face throbbed. She turned and spat blood onto his white pants.

"Next time, when I ask you to do something, you best do it."

Kenneth knelt and placed the torch on the floor, then wrapped both hands around the iron pole. The letters were glowing red.

"Once you have this on you, you're mine until the end of eternity."

"You can burn my entire body, and I'll still never be yours."

"You'll learn, just like all the others. You may be tougher to break, but that'll make the reward that much sweeter," he said, making a kissing face. "Get ready."

With the iron inches away, the heat was scorching. She sank back into the pillow, fixated on the ceiling, then bit down hard with her fists clenched, muscles tight.

As he eased the iron onto her thigh, the metal melted her flesh. She screamed, knowing no one would hear her.

Sometime later, Emily strolled into the room carrying a first aid kit. Hannah had made attempts at cleaning the wound with the dirty washcloth, but the blister was already half the size of a tomato, swollen and pus-filled. And with each movement there was a pain that she'd never felt before, even in her worst days of self-mutilation.

As much as she loathed taking help from anyone from Seven Day Saints—especially Emily—it becoming infected was a major concern, and she knew if the infection spread, it could lead to sepsis, and possible death.

"Let me see it," Emily said, sitting bedside.

Reluctantly, Hannah pulled off the sheets. Emily stared for a long moment.

"Wow, that is a doozy," she said, bobbing her head. "It's definitely going to take some time to heal, but when it does, it's going to be beautiful."

Hannah said nothing. There was nothing to say.

Emily opened the first aid kit and began removing supplies. Scissor, gauze pads, bandages, burn dressing, and a bottle of rubbing alcohol.

"This might sting a little," Emily said, soaking a gauze pad with the alcohol.

As she scrubbed the wound, Hannah's leg throbbed. She tried to conceal the pain, but it became unbearable, and she grimaced, feeling tears running down her cheek.

Emily stopped and glanced up. "I'm sorry Hannah,

and I know you probably hate this, but I promise, someday you'll look down at this scar and wonder how you ever lived without it."

All Hannah wanted was for her to stop talking. She couldn't stand to hear the sound of Emily's voice a moment longer. *Shut the fuck up*, she cried to herself. *Shut up! Shut up!* Emily gave a haunting smile like she could read Hannah's thoughts. Then returned to scrubbing the wound, this time with more pressure.

Looking at the back of Emily's head, Hannah imagined grabbing it and smashing it into the wall until she was bloody and unconscious. As much satisfaction as it'd bring her, she knew it would be a death sentence.

Emily secured the bandage, then glanced up. "I'll be back in a few hours to change this out. Try not to touch it or move too much. I'd hate for that thing to get infected."

SEVEN

Time ceased to exist. Day and night, sun and moon were no more. No rain, no snow, no clouds, no weather, no seasons. No television, or music, or games, or laughter. No voice other than her own.

In her weakest moments, Hannah wanted to scream, but she didn't for two reasons. One: if they heard, they'd suspect they were breaking her. Two: if she heard herself, she'd be certain they actually were.

Her body was deteriorating along with her mind. She was weak, very weak. She was wasting away, her muscles in a slow state of atrophy, so much so that walking to the bathroom was all the strength she could muster.

And even though she was lying in bed most of the day, she was at the point of exhaustion, probably never getting more than a few hours of sleep at a time without being jarred awake.

A single light hung from the middle of the ceiling, directly over the bed. It was always on. Always. Even with her eyes closed, she could see the light—the glow burned into her retinas. Sometimes she stared at the light and wished she'd fall asleep and never wake.

Sleep deprivation and seclusion were torture tactics. It wouldn't surprise her if they began waterboarding or introduced some form of electric shock. Hannah was losing her grasp on reality, and her sanity was gradually slipping away. This was all part of Kenneth's plan—break her down so he could mold her into what he wanted.

It only took two months for the Symbionese Liberation Army to brainwash Patty Hearst into robbing a bank with a semiautomatic rifle. Hannah was confident that she could last two months, but doubtful she could make six. A year, well, that would be almost impossible.

For meals, it was the same. Every day, every meal, breakfast and dinner. Two slices of white bread, one piece of bologna, a single piece of American cheese, probably a teaspoon of yellow mustard, served with a scoop of rice and a scoop of pinto beans. Hannah hated pinto beans, so every bite was a struggle to swallow, and if she hadn't been near starvation, she would've thrown them against the wall. But it was protein, and she knew that if she was ever going to escape, she would require every morsel of fuel available.

Around the eighth meal, Hannah found herself envying prison meal options, and around the fifteenth, she would've traded almost anything for a large piece of chocolate cake with an inch of frosting. That, along with a stiff whiskey and a cigarette, was what she daydreamed about. Mulling over what she'd have first if she ever escaped. After a strong internal back and forth, the final verdict was the cake while sipping on the whiskey, capping it with a cigarette.

Counting meals was how Hannah kept time. She calculated two meals a day, with breakfast around seven or eight and dinner probably ten to twelve hours later.

The same girl brought every meal. She gave it to Hannah, and then she would sit in one of the chairs and wait until Hannah was finished eating to retrieve the empty tray. She never spoke or made eye contact and ignored every question like she was a mute.

"What is your name?" Hannah asked on repeat, along with anything else she thought would get the girl to talk. "How old are you?", "What is your favorite color?", "What are your favorite hobbies?", and "What's your favorite food?" Nothing worked. Nothing. The girl never changed her facial expression or deviated from her routine. That didn't stop Hannah. She doubled down on the questions.

Bowel movements were few and far between. On the average, they occurred every eighth or ninth meal, so every four or five days. Always diarrhea. She assumed they were drugging her, maybe something to keep her docile.

Emily had chuckled when Hannah asked for an aspirin, telling her there was nothing of the sort, but thinking back, that was probably a lie. They wanted Hannah to suffer.

While searching the bathroom, Hannah found a three-inch bolt, and between feedings, she sharpened it against the bed frame until her forearms went numb. She continued until it was as sharp as a nail.

She decided if Kenneth ever got close enough, she'd grab him by the back of the neck, pull him down, then stab him with the makeshift blade until he was dead. It was most likely a death sentence for her as well, but at least her nightmare would be over, and just maybe, the stranglehold on the town would as well. Her life for thousands of people was a trade she'd be willing to make.

When Hannah had told her father that she was going to take Margaret and Steve's case, he'd turned silent for a moment, then let out a heavy sigh.

Finally, he said, "Are you sure you want to get involved?"

That was code for "Margaret doesn't give a fuck about you, and she only showed up at your door because she needed your help, so don't do her any favors." He was right, and Hannah should've listened.

She thought about how she might never see him again, and he'd be completely alone. With not one, but two dead children. He was a strong man, but that was something that most parents could never overcome, not even him. He'd told her as much.

He'd probably slip into a deeper alcoholic depression, drinking every waking moment until his liver failed from cirrhosis, landing him in the hospital on dialysis, but that wouldn't stop him. Then one day, a doctor would tell him. "Sorry, there's nothing else we can do for you," and he'd finally be at peace.

Hannah thought about Mark constantly. Where was he? What was he doing? Did he miss her as much as she missed him? Her thoughts always returning to that night in Capital Reef when he read *The Great Gatsby* aloud to her. Within the first few pages, she made a joke. "Will there be a test on this?"

He closed the book gently. "Shut up, Hannah. I'm going to read this to you, and you're going to like it. No, you're going to love it."

If she closed her eyes tight enough, she could hear his voice reading it back to her. And if not for those memories, she would've already run the nail across her wrist.

During the forty-sixth meal, the girl whispered. "I have something for you. Open your hand."

The girl slipped her hand into the pocket sewn onto

her dress. She remained completely still, studying Hannah. After about twenty seconds, she removed her hand and placed a piece of hard candy in the center of Hannah's palm.

"It's butterscotch. I hope you like it," the girl said.

Hannah nodded. By her best estimate, it'd been ten days since she'd heard a voice other than her own, and now she was speechless.

"You can't tell anyone I gave this to you, or else I'll get in serious trouble."

"Thank you, thank you," Hannah whispered, the words rushing out. "And I promise I won't."

The girl smiled weakly and looked at Hannah, holding her gaze for a moment before turning away as if averting her eyes from the sun.

"Please eat it now. I don't want anyone to find you with it."

Hannah placed the candy on her tongue and began sucking. It was euphoric, and she savored every swallow, never wanting it to dissolve. The girl watched for a minute, then slipped out of the room without saying another word.

For the next five meals, the girl waited until Hannah was finished eating, then gave her another piece of butterscotch candy. Hannah continued to ask questions, but the girl never said more than a few words, never divulging any personal information.

On the fifty-third trip, Hannah asked the girl's name once again, probably for the hundredth time. This time, the girl glanced up from the chair.

"Why do you want to know my name so much?"

"Because I'd personally like to thank you for the food you bring. If you didn't, I might not be alive."

The girl studied Hannah. "I, umm. I shouldn't tell you."

"I promise I won't tell anyone," Hannah whispered, holding her hand on her heart.

"Like I've said, I'll get into serious trouble if anyone catches me talking to you."

"Worse than this?"

She nodded. "Yes. Much, much worse."

Hannah thought about every word, not wanting to say anything that'd frighten the girl and have her return to the mute state.

"Then why did you decide to talk to me?"

"You seem nice. And I don't think it's fair they lock you up down here."

Hannah smiled. "You seem nice too."

The girl returned the smile. "Is your name really Tiffany?"

"No, that's an alias."

"Aliens?"

Hannah giggled. "Not aliens. Alias. It means a fake name."

"Oh," the girl said, drawn out. "Because you didn't want anyone in town knowing your real name."

"Yes, exactly."

"That's smart."

"My name is Hannah. Hannah Jacobs, and I'm from Colorado."

The girl rushed toward the bed and placed her palms on the mattress. "Is it really?"

"It is."

"Are you serious? My name is Anna." The girl chuckled. "Our names are almost exactly the same. Well, except for the two H's. That is so neat. I've never met anyone with my name, so you're the closest. Have you ever met anyone with yours?"

The name triggered a memory, but Hannah couldn't place it. "No, I haven't either."

"Awesome," she said with childlike enthusiasm. Her eyes were the purest blue Hannah had ever seen, like looking into glacier water. They were mesmerizing. "Colorado? That's east of Utah, right?" Anna pointed to the door.

"It is. They're neighbors."

"What is it like?"

"Mountains, some big cities, a football team that people die for, a lot of snow, cold winters, hot summers, and beautiful national parks."

"Does it have any big lakes?"

"No, nothing like Salt Lake."

"I've never seen Salt Lake. Have you?"

"Yeah, I've driven by it," Hannah said.

"Have you ever seen the ocean?"

"Have I seen the ocean?"

"Yes." The girl nodded feverishly, her eyes lit up. "Have you seen it?"

Her innocent demeanor brought a smile to Hannah's face, lifting her spirits.

"Yeah, I've been to the ocean a bunch of times."

"Which ones?" Anna said, leaning forward.

"The Pacific and Atlantic. I take it you've never been."

"No. I've only seen it in a few pictures. And I've asked everyone who lives here, and nobody, and I mean nobody, has said they've ever seen it. I think some people are lying, though. I don't know why you'd lie about something like that. If it was me, I'd be talking about it nonstop, and people would have to tell me to shut up." Anna paused for a moment, catching her breath. "Tell me everything about them."

"They are beautiful, and so majestic. Every time I see them, it's like the first time. I mean, in a sense it is, because the waves are never the same. One of my favorite things is sitting on the beach at sunset, sticking my feet in the sand, and listening to the waves crash into the shore."

Hannah told stories about being a kid, and visiting her grandma with Casey, but purposely omitted the story about being pulled in by the rip current and almost drowning. No need to bring up a traumatic childhood experience.

"Gosh, it sounds so amazing. Every night I go to bed praying I'll wake up next to the ocean, but every morning I wake up here," Anna said.

"Well, hopefully you'll get to go someday soon."

"I doubt it. It seems so far away. I've never really been outside of Washington County. And if I'm being honest, I haven't been farther than St. George," Anna said, giggling. "I was born here. I'll die here. And everything in between will be determined by Kenneth."

"It doesn't have to be that way."

After a short silence, Anna pushed off the bed. "I need to get going."

"See you tomorrow?"

With her lips sealed, Anna nodded. She picked up the tray, then left the room, never looking back.

The following meal, Anna handed Hannah the tray and sat down. "I'm sorry for running out of here last night. I never really talk about personal stuff with anyone, so it felt weird."

"What about your parents? Or siblings? Or friends?"

"I don't have any friends, and I don't really talk to my brothers, and I've never been close to my mom. And my dad, he umm, died when I was seven. An accident, he was working on a van in the garage and the jack gave out and it crushed him. About a week after the funeral, my mom married Douglas, the third-in-command at Seven Day."

Hannah had a strong suspicion the death wasn't an accident, and she bet if it was investigated, foul play would come to light.

"I was a daddy's girl, and I hate Douglas more than anyone except Kenneth, so I try to keep my distance from him and my mom."

"What has Douglas done to you?" Hannah asked, unsure if she was prepared for the answer.

"Oh, nothing like that. He has never laid a hand on me, but he forced me to marry his brother, Ronald. Well, with Kenneth's blessing."

"How old are you?"

"How old do I look?"

"You look like you're thirteen, but I looked like I was twelve until I was in my early twenties, so I'm going to guess high. Sixteen?"

"Almost. I'm seventeen."

The girl didn't have the mentality of someone about to become an adult, and definitely not one who should be married.

"And when did you marry him?"

"Three years ago. Exactly one week after my fourteenth birthday."

"How old is this fucking guy?"

"Forty-seven," Anna said with a lifeless smile. "And the funny thing is—well, you probably won't think it is funny, but one of his daughters is the ninth-grade teacher, so my homeroom teacher was my stepdaughter. It was a little weird at first, but after a few weeks, I didn't even think about it, I guess."

Hannah felt sick. These men were pure evil, and all of them deserved to die.

"Before the wedding, he barely made eye contact with me and never said more than a few words, and nothing changed after. I'm almost certain he reviled me, and the only times he treated me like his wife is when he wanted sex."

The thought of that man having his way with Anna sparked the same rage Hannah had felt when she spoke with Roxy.

"And you wanna know the worst part?" Anna said, twirling her thumbs.

"Worse than the rape? Sure."

"His smell. It was so gross, like he rolled around in manure all day. I almost threw up every time he took his clothes off." She paused, and a quick smile broke on her face. "Thank god I don't have to deal with that smell ever again."

"Why not?"

"He's dead. One afternoon he went on a walk, and he just dropped to the ground and died. They think it was a heart attack, but I don't know, I think I might be partially responsible."

"Why in the world would you think you're responsible?"

"Every day I prayed, and prayed, and prayed that he'd stop touching me, and finally, on that day, my prayers were answered."

If only it were that easy to kill monsters.

"You didn't kill him, I can promise you that. If anything, it was probably the guilt of being a vile human that came crashing down onto him."

With tears rolling down her face, Anna began to speak, but her voice was hollow. She wiped them away and cleared her throat.

"After he died, I went out about a mile into the canyon and screamed as loud as I could. I was so happy he was gone. In fact, I don't think I've ever been that happy before. I thought I was finally free, but three days ago, Kenneth called, and after he was finished with me, he told me I was scheduled to get married to Carl Morgan next week."

She cleared her throat again. "My second marriage. Lucky me—I'm going to have two husbands before I graduate high school."

"You can't marry this man, Anna. All of these men should be in jail for the rest of their lives," Hannah said.

"What other choice do I have?"

"You can leave."

Anna belted out a loud laugh, then quickly covered her mouth. "And go where? I don't know a single person outside of this town. Anyways, I'm pretty sure I'd get captured before I made it out of the city limits."

"You won't know unless you try," Hannah said.

"Nope, I'm trapped here, with Kenneth, and I know he'll never let me leave."

On the next visit, Hannah wanted to keep the conversation trivial. She was wary of scaring Anna away to the point that she'd stop bringing food, or would report Hannah to leadership at Seven Day Saints, or even worse, fall into territory that Hannah had experienced in her darkest days.

"What do you do around here for fun?" Hannah asked, taking a bite of a sandwich.

"Outside of my normal duties? I guess work."

"Most people don't consider work fun."

"Most people don't live in Echo Canyon."

"Good point. Where do you work?"

"I'm a waitress at Echo Cafe."

"I ate there. It's pretty good for a roadside diner. How do you like it?"

"It's cool. I mean, for people my age, it's one of the better jobs you could have. I get to meet some interesting people."

"Like who?"

"Tourists. Well, mostly hikers. I get to hear about all their adventures. This one guy who came in last summer was hiking from the South rim of the Grand Canyon to Yosemite. Something like five hundred miles, and for almost three straight months. And he was in his seventies! Gosh, he was so nice. He showed me the route on the map and gave me some hiking advice. I was so grateful for the conversation, I gave him a complimentary slice of bumbleberry pie."

"Bumbleberry pie? So weird, I'd never heard that until I came down here."

"Really? It's like world-famous down around these parts."

Hannah was about to take another bite, then stopped. It finally hit her, and she realized who Anna was, and cursed herself for taking so long. Maybe it was the lack of sleep, or the lack of food, or the lingering effect of the concussion, or maybe it was as simple as that she wasn't as sharp as she once had been.

"Wait a minute, you're the girl who gave the reporter the note warning him to leave, aren't you?" Hannah said, pointing at Anna.

Anna looked away. "What reporter?"

"Last year, a reporter from the *Salt Lake Times* was in town, and when he was at the diner, a waitress slipped him a note, warning him to leave town. Was that you?"

"Umm, I don't know what you're talking about."

Even the worst card player had a better poker face than Anna.

"You realize part of my job is to tell if someone is lying, and I don't think I've ever seen anyone worse than you."

Anna sighed and rolled her eyes. "Yes, it was me. I overheard Kenneth say that he shouldn't be here, and was worried they were going to do something, so I slipped him the note."

"That was very brave."

Anna started to blush. "I didn't really think about it. I would've done the same for you."

"So, you might've saved him from something like this, or worse."

"I don't know what they were planning. I think even Kenneth knows that kidnapping a reporter for a major newspaper isn't a good idea. People would've come looking for him."

"I was a little easier to make disappear."

"Yeah, kind of. Sorry."

"It's fine, I walked right into their trap," Hannah said with a soft smile.

"Besides being a waitress, what else do you do?"

"I don't know."

"Come on, that isn't an answer. There has to be something that you like doing outside of work."

"Well, I play a little guitar. Kenneth gave me some lessons a few years back. It was the only good thing he has ever done for me. I'm not very good, but it makes me happy."

"That's the most important thing. Who is your favorite band?"

"You're not going to make fun?"

"I pinky swear," Hannah said, extending her right hand.

"We're not allowed to listen to music, so I've really only heard what Kenneth plays on his guitar. The Beatles, Pink Floyd, and I think the Rolling Stones. There are some songs that are okay, but I don't really enjoy most of it. Maybe the records are better than Kenneth." She paused for a moment, thinking. "Oh, and I've heard the music at the dances, but I don't really like that, yuck."

She looked up at Hannah, and her face shifted. "If I tell you something, do you promise to keep it a secret?"

Hannah nodded.

"Last year, I was in this clothing store in St. George, and there was this song they played over the speakers, and I instantly fell in love with it. I asked an employee who it was, and I guess it was a song called 'Fake Plastic Trees' by a band called Radiohead." She shrugged. "On the drive back here, I tried my hardest to remember the music, and the second I got home, I picked up my guitar and played it as best as I could from memory. I'm sure my version sounds nothing like what I heard in the store, though," Anna said.

"So, would you say Radiohead is your favorite band?"

"I guess you could say that."

"You wanna know something?"

"Of course."

"That is one of my favorite songs from one of my favorite bands."

"You're joshing me again!"

"I promise, I'll never lie to you."

"Really?"

"I swear on everything, Anna."

Anna's face lit up.

"Look at that! I think that is one of the biggest smiles I've ever seen." Hannah sat up and kicked off the sheets.

"Oh my gosh." Anna's eyes went wide, and the color disappeared from her face.

"What's wrong?" Hannah said, but as the words rolled off her tongue, she realized Anna was peering down at the countless scars scattered across her thighs. Humiliation washed over her, and she jerked the sheets to her stomach.

Anna looked into Hannah's eyes, then stood and unfastened her dress, letting it fall to the floor. "I thought I was the only one," she said, caressing the scars surrounding the Seven Day Saints brand on her upper thigh.

Hannah fixated on the scars out of morbid curiosity, like staring at a car crash. "You did all of those?"

Anna nodded. "I had a hunch that Kenneth would be disgusted by them, and I was right. He actually loathes them, said each one is a sin. The first time he saw them, I got the worst beating of my life. Two black eyes and some bruised ribs, but it was worth it, because now he only touches me when he's really, really drunk." Anna cleared her throat. "Why did you do yours?"

"I started when I was around your age, after my sister Casey was murdered."

Anna covered her mouth and whispered, "I'm so sorry."

"She was my best friend, my entire world. When she died, a big piece of me died. I was in a dark place, and it was hard to go on, but last year, I caught her killer, and it feels like the scars are becoming a distant memory, and I'm hopeful that one day I'll be healed."

"Do you think someday I'll be able to say that? That I'm healed?" Anna asked.

"If you escape this place, I promise it will happen."

Anna nodded, and then the room got quiet for a long time.

Finally, Anna said, "We're friends, right?"

"Yeah, of course we're friends."

"That makes me happy. Like I've said, I don't really have any friends, and as pathetic as it sounds, I talk to you more than anyone." She let out a nervous laugh. "And you probably know me better than anyone else."

The girl was completely alone, just like Hannah after Casey's murder.

"Now that we're friends, if I ask a question, will you be honest with me?" Hannah said.

"Yes."

"What is going to happen to me?"

Anna shifted her weight on the bed. "I don't know."

"How long are they going to keep me in this room?"

"I don't know."

"Are they going to kill me?"

"I don't know," Anna whispered. "I really don't."

Much later, the door opened and Anna slipped into the room again, closing it behind her with precision. She stared at Hannah, fighting back tears.

"What's wrong, Anna?" Hannah said sharply.

"I lied to you," Anna said.

"About what?"

"When you asked if I knew what is going to happen to you." Anna closed her eyes and took a deep breath. "Well, two nights ago, I overheard Kenneth and Douglas talking, and I couldn't hear everything, but it sounds like they were tipped off that the FBI is investigating your disappearance, and planning on coming to Echo Canyon."

"Wait, back up a second. The FBI is coming here?"

"Yes, and Kenneth is scared that if they find evidence you were here, they could get a search warrant and execute a raid. So, they want you gone."

"Did you hear what they plan to do with me?"

"They were going back and forth, but it sounded like they're either moving you to Mexico," she said, her voice dropping to a whisper. "Or umm, possibly the reeducation center."

"I take it that's not somewhere I want to be sent to."

"I've only heard rumors, but supposedly it's a cabin in the middle of the desert, like twenty miles south of here, and people who go there never return."

From the moment Hannah came to, she'd been certain this day was coming—it was inevitable. The only thing that had kept her spirits up was the possibility of escape, but now, she was the walking dead. Like an inmate on death row counting the days until they were strapped to the electric chair.

Growing up, Hannah hadn't cared about death. You're born, you live, you die. A blink of the eye in the galaxy. She always thought she'd die young, never seeing thirty. Definitely not seeing her forties, and she was fine with that. Never wanting to grow old.

Forty was the age, she decided, the body started to have diminishing returns. Put on a few pounds every year, varicose veins start to show, vision gets worse, hair begins turning gray. Then, around retirement, that's when the body completely falls apart. Memory lapses, incontinence, and the elevated risk of testing positive for countless cancers. Nope, not for her. Die young, and leave a good-looking corpse.

But being alone in this room, being so close to the end, made her realize she didn't want to die. She wanted to grow old, but instead, just like Casey, she'd never laugh or smile again, or see another sunset, or see another waterfall, or hear the ocean waves, or smell another flower.

Besides Mark and her father, the smell of flowers was

what she'd miss the most. Damn it, she'd really miss that. What she wouldn't do to smell the blooming of a spring lilac.

Hannah swallowed hard. "I guess my days are numbered then," she muttered.

Anna tiptoed to the bed and knelt in front of her. "No, I'm not going to let that happen. We're going to escape tonight."

"I can't let you do that, Anna. If they catch us, you …"

"If we get caught, I already know what's going to happen to me. They'll ship me away, and I'll be locked up for years, but it's worth it to me." Anna paused. "You're my friend, and I'm willing to take that risk."

"I don't want you to do this just for me, because whatever happens, your life will never be the same."

"I've been ready for a long time."

At that moment, the ceiling light began to flicker, and they both looked up. Something spiritual came over Hannah, and she was certain Anna felt the same.

"We leave tonight. I spent most of last night planning it out." Anna said.

"Let's hear what you got." Hannah sat up.

"I've already taken four Valium from Kenneth's personal stash. I'm going to crush them up, and as I'm preparing his dinner, I'll mix them into his mashed potatoes. That should knock him out until the morning. I'll lock his door, then grab the handcuff key from the security room and come down here and release you."

"Very good start."

Anna smiled. "After we get out of here, we'll go to the barn, grab my horse Bella, and ride out through Echo Canyon to the highway. There's a mining facility just north of where the canyon meets 99. It operates twenty-four hours a day, every day of the year. There are semitrucks coming in and out, all day and night, and when they leave, they're always heading west to St. George and I-15."

"What do we do when we get to the mining facility?"

"Tell them your abusive husband kicked us out of the car and we need a ride to a friend's house in St. George. One of those truckers will give us a ride, I just know it."

"And you think that would be better than telling the truth?"

"I went back and forth with that part, but on the off chance that one of the workers knows about Seven Day, or they call 911, and the responding officer has ties to Echo Canyon. Well, I don't want to be returned right back here. I think telling them you're an abused wife and I'm your kid sister gives us the best chance to get a ride without getting asked a bunch of questions."

Hannah nodded. "I do have one piece that I'm uncertain about, and excuse me for my ignorance. Wouldn't it be easier to just take a car and drive out of here instead of riding a horse through the canyon?"

"Well, even if we could make it past the guard station, which we can't—"

"Shit, I forgot about the guards."

Anna continued. "And were able to get a car, someone would most likely see us, and we'd probably only make it a few miles before someone caught up with us. Last year, Mary Todd stole a van, and members of Seven Day caught up with her about halfway to Red Mesa. They were about to run her off the road before she finally pulled over."

"So, a horse it is."

"It isn't all that bad. I've ridden through the canyon about a dozen times. It only takes like an hour to make it to the highway. If everything goes to plan, we should be heading to St. George before anyone knows were missing."

"What about the guards outside the door?" Hannah

said, pointing. "Emily said they're out there twenty-four seven."

"They're not anymore. They were there for like the first few weeks, and that's why I didn't talk. I think once they realized you weren't going to try to escape, they left. Occasionally, they'll take a peek down the stairs, but for the most part, they don't come around."

"And there are no other guards?"

"Not on the compound. They're more concerned about the guard station and who comes and goes in town."

"Are there cameras? Or any type of surveillance equipment?"

Anna smiled and shook her head. "No. We don't have anything like that."

"So, if I was able to get out of these handcuffs, I just walk up the stairs, out the back door, and off to freedom."

"Technically, yes."

"Sounds like they aren't that smart."

"Just because Kenneth is in charge doesn't mean he's competent."

The longer Hannah thought, the more she decided that it might just work, and she herself probably couldn't have come up with a better plan. The girl wasn't as innocent and naive as she seemed.

"And you're confident that we won't get caught?" Hannah said.

"Not completely, but what other options do we have?"

"If they catch you helping me escape, your fate will be tied to mine."

"I know," Anna said. "I'm prepared for that. Are you?"

EIGHT

On what would've been the fifty-eighth meal, Anna entered the room. Instead of carrying a tray, she wore a backpack and a heavy winter coat. Under her arm was another jacket. She sat next to Hannah, then offered a quick smile.

"Before I left my room, I was just sitting on my bed, trying to talk myself out of this, and I tried to think of what I was going to miss, and outside of you and Bella, I couldn't think of anything. Not a single thing. I'm just scared that I don't know if where I'm going is better or worse."

"I promise you, wherever you end up will be better than here."

Anna stared at the ground for a long time, then slowly turned to Hannah. "I guess I'm ready to leave this darn place. Sorry about the profanity."

Hannah laughed. "It's fine. And actually, could you repeat that, but instead of darn place, could you say fucking place?"

Anna turned bright red. "I can't say that."

"Yes, you can. Fucking, fucking, fucking. See it's that easy."

Twice Anna started to speak, but stopped. Then, barely a whisper, she said, "I'm ready to leave this fucking place."

Anna looked up to Hannah, seeking approval. Hannah smiled, then leaned in and kissed her on the forehead.

"That sounded fucking perfect."

The girl smiled. "I was able to find your shoes," Anna said, removing a pair of Chuck Taylors from her backpack.

"You're a rockstar! Thank you, thank you," Hannah said, and repeated it at least five more times.

The thought of crossing the desert in winter at night, on horseback, in sock feet was not something Hannah was looking forward too.

"Now for a coat, I only have my extra one."

Hannah slipped the coat on. It was snug, but it'd do. "What else did you bring?" she asked.

"Three bottles of water, three cans of peaches, and five apples. And I raided the rest of these from Kenneth's personal stash," Anna said, offering up a Snickers.

Without saying a word, Hannah snatched the candy bar and devoured it like a kid eating their first piece of candy on Halloween. Never in her life had she eaten anything that fast. As she swallowed the last bite, she worried about becoming sick, but after a dozen deep breaths, she was confident it would stay down.

"Oh my god, thank you so much, I really needed that," Hannah said, wiping chocolate off her lips. "Now I think I'm ready. What about you?"

Anna looked up, seemingly praying to the rivets in the ceiling. "As ready as I'll ever be."

Reaching into the backpack, she removed a key and unlocked the handcuff. Hannah examined her swollen wrist.

"Are you sure you still want to do this? It's not too

late for you to turn back." Hannah said, beginning to second-guess their plan herself.

If they got caught, Hannah already knew her fate, she wasn't coming back to the room, never. She'd commit suicide by any means possible, *but what would happen to Anna?* She'd probably be locked away for years. Easier not to think about what would happen if they failed.

Anna held the key between them, both of them staring at it. Then she tossed it into the bathroom, and it bounced off the wall twice, before coming to a rest on the cement floor.

"Before we go, I just have to do one last thing," Anna said. She removed a black magic marker and walked to the wall, then began scribbling over "Love Thy Brother and Sister." When the words were no longer legible, she took a step back and admired her work.

"Want to add anything?" Anna said, holding up the marker.

"No. That's perfect."

Anna dropped the marker, then kicked it across the floor. "I think I'm ready."

As Hannah staggered to the door, her legs started to buckle, having not walked more than a few steps in weeks. Anna reached out and grabbed her at the last second, and held her up until she could brace herself against the wall. Hannah looked down at Anna, realizing she was stronger than she appeared.

"Are you okay? I should've warned you that your legs might be weak." Anna said.

Hannah nodded feverishly. "Yeah, I probably should've done some stretching before you came."

Anna smiled, but it wasn't a smile of joy, it was one of fear and uncertainty. "Outside this door is another room, then a hallway that leads to a set of stairs. Once we make it to the top, there's a fake wall that leads into the storage room, and that leads into the office. We'll make a left, then go down the hallway to the back door. From there, it's about fifty feet to the barn."

"I hope there isn't going to be a test on this."

"I know, it's a bit of a maze."

"I guess that's how it stays hidden. How many stairs?" Hannah asked, trying to make a mental image.

"Like twenty, I guess."

Hannah burned the route into her memory. Room, twenty stairs, a storage room, office, then a hallway to the back door and on to the barn.

Reaching back, Anna found Hannah's hand and squeezed. "I'm scared," she murmured.

"We're going to be okay," Hannah said. Then she took the deepest breath she'd ever taken and held it, like she was preparing for an underwater swim.

Anna placed her hands on the door and carefully pushed it open. She stepped through the doorway, and Hannah followed. The connecting room was about twice the size and on the far wall were four metal gun safes that were at least three feet wide and six feet tall. If each safe was stocked, it'd be enough to start a small war. Hannah stared for a moment, then turned to the stairs.

As they traversed the rickety steps, each one creaked louder than the last, and seemingly echoed throughout the stairway. Twice Anna stopped and remained completely still for ten, maybe twenty seconds. Each time they stopped, Hannah feared she'd fall and clutched the railing for dear life.

With five steps remaining, there was the faint sound of a TV show theme song, but Hannah couldn't quite place it.

Hannah leaned in to Anna and whispered, "Where is that coming from?"

"Kenneth's room. It's a few doors down."

"Do we have to walk past it?"

Anna nodded.

"Lovely," Hannah whispered.

"Sorry, it is the shortest way to the back door."

"It's fine. I just wasn't prepared for it. Hopefully he'll be knocked out until next week."

When they reached the top of the stairs, Hannah turned back and let out a sigh. Phase one complete. *Celebrate the small victories.* Now only about ten other things needed to go perfectly, and they'd be in St. George.

Anna looked over her shoulder, doubt flooding her eyes. "Let's try to go as fast as we can." She squeezed Hannah's hand and led her through the office. At the doorway, she peered in both directions.

"All clear," Anna whispered.

Hannah staggered down the hallway like she'd drunk a half bottle of whiskey. Almost falling twice, both times catching herself on the wall.

"Try to be quiet—I don't want anyone to hear us," Anna said.

The longer Hannah was on her feet, the weaker they became, and the more she worried. "I'm trying, but my legs are not cooperating."

Placing a hand on Anna's shoulder, Hannah followed her every step, like she was trudging behind in the snow and didn't want to leave a single fresh track.

As they crept down the hall, Hannah became dizzy. Each time she glanced at the doorknob to Kenneth's room, she swore she saw it move ever so slightly.

Hannah leaned in. "Is there any chance that someone else could be in his room?"

Turning halfway, Anna said, "I don't, umm, think so."

Not the response Hannah wanted to hear. "I sure hope not," she whispered, squeezing Anna's shoulder.

Their strides shortened as they neared the door, and the floorboards creaked louder and louder. Every step felt heavier than the last, and Hannah was terrified one would sink to the floor like an anchor and wake Kenneth or alert someone.

At Kenneth's door, they stopped, and in unison they turned to it. If Hannah had the strength, she would've kicked it down and strangled the life out of him. Instead, she spat on it.

As they continued, their pace increased, and for the first time since entering the hallway, Hannah was certain they were going to make it to the back door. Twenty feet, ten feet, five, four, and then it was at arm's length.

"If you're not careful, this will slam shut and wake up the entire town."

They exchanged a fear-laden glance, then both nodded.

"Let's go," Anna said.

She carefully pushed on the door, then gestured Hannah through. For a moment, Hannah thought she'd step outside and be surrounded by Kenneth and his army, and any chance of escape would be over, and she'd be thrown back into the dungeon.

She closed her eyes, then slipped through the opening. The cold air on her face was a shock, something she hadn't even realized she'd missed. After a deep breath, Hannah slowly opened her left eye, then her right.

No one. Not a single person. In front of her was the barn, the canyon walls, the sky, the moon, and home. Hannah wanted to drop to her knees and kiss the ground, but she feared if she did, she wouldn't be able to get back up.

Glancing skyward, Hannah shed a tear. The stars were a sight she'd thought she'd never see again, and they were as brilliant as she remembered. They illuminated like streetlights, and even though they were millions of years away, they felt like they were within reach. A light rain began to fall as Hannah gazed upon Orion the Hunter.

"Sorry to interrupt your stargazing," Anna said, "but we probably should get to the barn before someone sees us."

In the barn were about a dozen stalls, with a horse in each one. As they walked across the dirt-and-hay-covered floor, the horses silently watched their every step. At the fourth stall, Anna stopped and leaned in. The horse approached her, and she started massaging its neck.

"Here is the girl who's going to help us escape," Anna said, pressing her forehead against the horse's nose.

"I take it this is Bella."

Anna nodded. "She's a good girl, aren't you Bella. My bestest friend."

"She's beautiful. Can I touch her?"

"Of course. You guys are going to become fast friends."

Carefully Hannah raised her hand, letting Bella see it. Then she leaned in and began stroking her mane. Bella gently huffed through her nostrils.

"Don't be scared. We're going to make it out together," Hannah said.

"You're going to need this," Anna said, holding out a riding helmet.

Hannah thanked her, then put it on and adjusted the straps.

"I just realized it's going to be pitch black out there. Do you have a flashlight or headlamp or anything?"

Anna shook her head. "Light in these canyons can travel for miles. No light means we won't be able to see much, but that also means no one else will see it either. I don't want someone going to their kitchen and getting a glass of water and seeing lights in the canyon walls. They'd for sure call the guard station, and once that happens, they'd find Kenneth comatose, and discover you were missing, and the jig would be up."

"Great, so we're doing this blind."

"Don't worry, Bella is all the eyes we need. She's done this multiple times. Huh girl? You're going to get us to the highway just fine. I know you are," Anna said. "And if I'm being honest, some of the ride is scary, so it might be better if you can't see."

"What's going to happen to her when we get to the highway?"

"It's her time to escape this place too," Anna said. "She was wild when we got her, and I was the only one who was able to tame and ride her. Without me here, she wouldn't serve a purpose, so I'm sure Kenneth would have someone put a bullet in her head the moment he knew I was gone." Anna wiped away tears with her sleeve, then kissed Bella. "There are wild horses all over this area, and it might take a minute, but her instincts will kick back in, and she'll find a new pack. I just know it."

"I'm sure she'll be okay," Hannah said, her voice cracking. Bella was Anna's only true friend, and she was about to sacrifice that friendship to save Hannah.

The barn fell silent. Then, as if to signal she was ready, Bella blew a loud snort. Both of them started to laugh.

"It sounds like Bella is ready to go. Are you?" Anna said.

"Yeah, umm, I don't know if this is an important detail or not, but I've never ridden a horse before."

Anna cocked her head. "Well, I've finally found something I've done that you haven't."

"And after seeing her, I'm somewhat terrified. I wasn't expecting her to be so ..." Hannah opened her arms as wide as she could. "Big."

Anna giggled. "There is nothing to worry about. Bella is going to do all the work. The only thing you have to do is hold on to me as tight as you can."

"I'm going to warn you now that I'll probably squeeze the life out of you."

"Do whatever you have to do," Anna said, extending her hand.

Hannah took it, then leaned in to Bella and kissed her. "Thank you in advance for the ride."

Soon they were deep into the canyon. Hannah wasn't prepared for the violent headwind, and as the temperature dropped, she tightened her grip around Anna, her fingers interlocked and frozen. She had no idea how fast they were going, or in what direction, or what time it was, or how far it was until the highway.

The sky cast a blue light, shining down onto the canyon floor. It must've looked nearly identical when travelers explored this region hundreds or even thousands of years ago.

As they put distance between themselves and Kenneth and everyone that wanted to harm them, Hannah's confidence grew. Maybe they would make it out. Maybe they'd be able to tell their story of the horror that occurred at Echo Canyon.

At a fork in the canyon, Anna pulled up on Bella. When they stopped, a cloud of dust settled, disappearing quickly. Anna looked to the left, then right, then back to the left, then again to the right, as Bella shifted in place.

"How long do you think we've been riding?" Hannah said.

"If I had to guess, like twenty minutes."

A third of the way, Hannah thought. After wiping dirt out of her eyes, she watched as Anna continued to survey the land. Then she realized Anna was lost, and her stomach sank. "Do you know what way to go?"

"Yeah, I'm just trying to think. I'm pretty sure, umm, no. It is to the left."

"You're the expert," Hannah said, not wanting to cast doubt on the choice.

Anna nodded, then shouted, "Come on, Bella!"

Shortly after they passed the fork, a roaring boom rattled the canyon. Terror coursed throughout Hannah's body. Her first thought was that someone had discovered they were missing and was in pursuit. Maybe it was a car engine or a gun shot. Cautiously, she peered back, but she saw nothing but a black void. No headlights, no flashlights, no sign of anyone.

"What the fuck was that?" Hannah said.

"I don't know! Hold on tight."

Hannah wasn't sure if she could hold on any tighter without choking Anna.

The noise became louder, and louder, and louder. Hannah kept turning back, but each time she saw nothing.

Anna pulled up on Bella and glanced over her shoulder. "Can you see anything?"

"No, nothing!" Hannah yelled.

"I'm going to head over there to get a better view," Anna said, pointing to a ledge.

The hair on Hannah's arms stood straight up, and an energy shot through her entire body that she'd never felt, one that she couldn't explain. Maybe this was what someone experienced just before getting struck by lightning.

As they started to the ledge, a boom as loud as a freight train echoed off the canyon walls, engulfing them. Anna yelled something, but it was pointless—Hannah couldn't even hear herself think.

Within seconds, and before they could react, all three of them were airborne. It happened so fast, like crossing an intersection and seeing another vehicle run a red light, seconds from an impending crash. No time to react, just enough time to realize what was about to happen.

Hannah hung in the air for what felt like seconds, and as she fell back down to earth, she saw a glimpse of water rushing across the canyon floor. She stretched her hand out, knowing it was hopeless. Nothing was going to protect her.

When Hannah opened her eyes, the water was rushing across her chest. It was freezing—a cold she'd never experienced, and one she hadn't thought existed in a liquid form. There was a shooting pain in her abdomen, and she was having trouble breathing, but as far as she could tell, no broken bones or life-threatening injuries.

Her back was against Bella's, who was acting as a makeshift sandbag, and she faced the oncoming current. Each time she tried to move, the weight of the water kept her grounded. If she had landed face down, the current might've kept her submerged, and she probably would've never taken another breath.

Her thoughts quickly turned to Anna. Where was she? Did she get swept away? Frantically, she began searching for her. "Anna!" she yelled repeatedly.

Over the sound of the water, she faintly heard the girl cry, "I'm back here!"

Hannah turned around and saw the top of Anna's head. She was on the other side of Bella, between the horse's legs.

"Are you okay?" Hannah shouted.

"I don't know. My leg really hurts."

"Is it broken?"

"I don't know. Maybe."

"Hold on, I'm coming over!"

As she was preparing to climb over Bella, a piece of debris, probably a tree branch, slammed into her chest, knocking the wind out of her for the second time in minutes. Struggling to catch her breath, she finally coughed, spitting out a mixture of saliva and blood.

"Hannah! Are you hurt?"

"I'm fine, I'm fine," Hannah said, spitting out more blood with the words.

She arched her back, then dug her heels into the mud and pushed and pushed and pushed. It was useless. Like she was wearing a weighted vest.

"Fuck," she screamed, hitting the water with closed fists.

After taking a moment to pull herself together, she took a few deep breaths, then squirmed until she had enough momentum to roll onto her stomach. Once there, Hannah bent her knees, and just as she was about to push off, a new fear was unlocked. What if she thrust herself with such force that she was catapulted back into the raging water, and the current swept her away from Anna?

"When I come over, try to grab me," Hannah yelled.

She pushed off and the water hurled her over Bella, dropping her hard onto her shoulder.

"I got you! I got you!" Anna screamed, digging her nails into Hannah's bicep.

After sitting up, Hannah said, "Let me see your leg."

Anna raised it, and her ankle hung limp, dangling in the air.

"That does not look good," Hannah muttered.

It was broken, without a doubt, and depending on the severity of the break, there might be torn tendons as well.

Anna looked at it for a second longer, then turned to Bella. "I think Bella is hurt. She's having a hard time breathing."

Bella's breathing had indeed become erratic, and her eyes began to roll back. Hannah feared a life-threatening injury from when she landed. If that was the case, there was nothing Hannah or Anna could do to save her.

"You're going to be okay, Bella," Anna said, rubbing her belly. "Come on girl, come on, you can make it."

With their hands on Bella, they remained still and silent for a long time. Finally, needing to distract herself, Hannah stood and surveyed the terrain. Less than twenty feet to the left was a rock ledge that was bone dry. Hannah was certain she could carry Anna there, and at least they'd be safe for the moment.

"I hate leaving Bella, but I think we should get to higher ground."

"I'm not leaving her side."

"Okay. We'll stay put as long as the water doesn't rise, but if it does, we'll have to get up there," Hannah said.

Anna nodded, never taking her eyes off Bella.

Hannah watched the water for a long time. The level seemed to be diminishing, but that didn't guarantee a second round wasn't already barreling down the canyon, and if that happened, they might not be so lucky again.

When she could no longer stand, she sat down, resting her head between her knees. Exhaustion was setting in at a level Hannah had never felt. If she hadn't been in fear for her life, she probably could have fallen asleep right there.

Hannah untied her shoes, took off her socks, and wrung them out about ten times each. They were still wet, but at least they weren't soaked. She set them on a rock, then turned to Anna.

"Let's see that ankle again," Hannah said. Since she last examined it, the swelling had nearly doubled.

"We need to get this boot off. It might hurt a little."

"Do it," Anna said, brushing the hair out of her eyes.

After untying her shoe, Hannah removed the laces. "Are you ready?"

Anna nodded, then bit her bottom lip and looked up

to the cloudless sky. Like ripping off a Band-Aid, Hannah yanked off the shoe. Anna whimpered, her leg quivering in Hannah's hands.

"I'm so sorry."

"It's okay," Anna said.

Hannah took off the other shoe, then rolled off her socks and wrung them out as well before giving them back to Anna.

"I think it's best if you don't put one back on that ankle. Keeping it off will reduce pressure on it."

They remained completely still. Anna whimpered, and Hannah watched the water start to recede. The night sky was as dark as ever, providing no hint to what time it was. And time was not on their side, because she knew come daylight, they'd be visible to the world, and if Kenneth came looking for them in the canyon, they'd be as good as caught.

After some time, Hannah said, "We have to leave."

Anna didn't acknowledge her. Hannah repeated "We have to leave" five more times before placing her hand on Anna's shoulder. "I know you don't want to leave Bella, but if we don't, we might not make it out of here. You're hurt. You need a doctor."

"Just a little longer," Anna mumbled.

Even though Hannah felt like they couldn't remain, she waited for what felt like five more minutes. Just as she was about to tell Anna they had to leave for the final time, Bella went into convulsions.

"Bella! Bella!" Anna screamed.

The horse flailed, and then her breathing grew even more shallow. She looked directly into Anna's eyes, as if saying goodbye, then slowly closed them. Moments later, Bella took her last breath.

"No, no, no!" Anna cried.

For a long time, she didn't move, remaining cheek to cheek with Bella.

"I'm so sorry Anna, but there's nothing you can do for her now."

Through her tears, Anna released Bella, then turned toward Hannah and nodded gravely. Hannah reached out to help her stand, but Anna swatted her away. She rose on one leg, and after teetering for a few seconds, she gathered her balance.

Anna placed a hand on Bella's stomach and cleared her throat. "Bella, you're the best thing that has ever happened to me, and I'm going to miss you more than life itself. You traded your life for ours, and I'll never forget that. I hope wherever you're going, you get to run free, and hopefully someday I'll get to ride you again."

They remained in silence for almost a minute, and then Anna reached to Hannah. "I'm ready, but I'm not going to be able to walk."

"I know. I'm going to carry you."

"You're going to carry me?"

"Yes, I'm not going to leave you here, and there's no way you could do it on one leg. How far do you think the highway is?"

"If I had to guess, I'd say about two or three miles."

Hannah started to do the math. At a normal hiking pace, she averaged about twenty minutes a mile. But exhausted, injured, and with Anna on her back, she estimated it was going to take three to four times that. And that was if they didn't make a wrong turn, and if they didn't run into a debris field that they'd have to climb. And if they came upon one that was impassable, well, that'd be the end of their journey.

"That's nothing! We'll be in St. George before sunrise," Hannah said.

Anna gave a weak smile, but by the look on her face, Hannah knew she didn't believe her. Fuck, she barely believed herself.

"I promise I won't stop until we are out of here. You believe me, right?"

Anna nodded.

"No, I need to hear you say it. Do you believe me?"

Hannah was almost certain they were going to die in that canyon, but she held on to a tiny sliver of hope that they'd make it out. But if Anna didn't believe it, Hannah would lose faith, and she wouldn't have the will to continue on.

"Yes, I believe you," Anna cried.

"Good. Now get on my back and let's get going."

Anna slipped on the backpack, then placed her hands onto Hannah's shoulders and climbed on piggyback style. As Hannah stood, she teetered forward, but she quickly caught herself. After three deep breaths, she rose again and took one small step. Then another, and another. Then they set off into the canyon.

Almost as fast as the raging water had arrived, it was nearly gone, leaving behind a newly formed stream littered with tree branches, rocks, vegetation, and mud. The landscape, once dry and dead, now showed the tiniest bit of life—and the water most likely would flow to the highway, a sign showing them the way. Despite their dire situation, the sound of the water was soothing, helping calm Hannah's nerves. Without it, she might've had a full-blown panic attack.

As she walked, Hannah struggled to breathe. Maybe a broken rib. She prayed it wasn't a kidney laceration or internal bleeding.

"Do you think we're going to die tonight?" Anna asked.

Hannah stopped and thought for a moment. With a labored voice, she said, "No. It's going to take longer than we thought, but we're going to make it out."

"Okay. Because if you think we're going to die, I'll ask you to take me back to Bella, so I can lie next to her."

"I promise I will," Hannah said, trying to hold her voice together. If she'd been alone, she would've given up, but as long as Anna was alive, she was not going to stop.

Her shoes and socks were water-logged, making each step twice as hard. And the mud, so much mud. It was inches deep in some spots, and when it dried, it felt like her ankles and calves were covered in plaster.

The terrain would have been a challenge for seasoned explorers, but it was near impossible for someone wearing a dress and Chuck Taylors and carrying a teenage girl. She studied the canyon in front of them, then turned back from where they'd come from. It all looked exactly the same. They could've been going in a circle and Hannah would've been none the wiser.

"I'm hungry," Anna said, barely above a whisper.

Hannah gently placed her down on a flat boulder and handed her a Snickers and a bottle of water.

"Here, drink this. You need it," Hannah said.

After two bites, Anna offered some to Hannah. She took a nibble, then gave it back. While Anna finished the candy bar, Hannah worked off her shoes with her swollen sausage fingers.

"That's not good," Hannah whispered.

Some time ago, she'd felt a strange sensation in the back of her heels, and had been unsure if it was her imagination or something else. Well, it was something else. They were raw—the skin completely gone. As she cleaned them with a dirty sock, they pulsated bright red.

Without proper first aid, the wound would get worse, and there'd be a chance her flesh would open all the way to the bone. If that occurred, neither of them would be able to walk, and they'd be as good as dead.

Sometimes she found herself wishing the flood had swept them away. A quick and easy death. Not like this. Not a slow and agonizing demise.

Hannah remembered a story of a ten-year-old-girl who'd survived ten days without food or water in the ruins of an apartment building after an earthquake in the Philippines. Doctors and experts had been unsure how she possibly survived that long. Maybe her will to live was stronger than Hannah's.

They sat for a long time—a very long time. The longer they remained there, the more content Hannah felt. Warmth overcame her, like she was at home, in bed, and under a mountain of covers.

"Should we ... get going?" Anna whispered, her voice reminiscent of a dream.

But a different voice was telling Hannah to remain still. Keep her eyes closed, and just rest for a little longer. Everything was going to be fine.

Lying there, she felt nothing. Not the pain in her ankles, or her abdomen. Or the blisters on her feet, or her throbbing shoulders and back. For the first time in a long time, she was at peace.

Then she felt a nudge on her shoulder, and when Hannah opened her eyes, Anna was by her side, tapping her.

"Hannah ... I really think we should ... keep going," Anna said, her voice quivering.

Hannah stared for a moment, then gazed upon the night sky. The stars were gone, like they'd been erased. "Yeah, sorry, I just needed to rest for a second." She sat up and started wiping the mud off the back of her head and neck.

When they continued, dread crept in as the sky hung heavy, like it was going to collapse down on them.

"Bella saved my life," Anna said wearily. "I thought I was carrying Kenneth's child, and I wasn't about to have his kid. So, I decided I was going to end everything. After everyone went to bed one night, I took a straight razor from the medicine cabinet and started to write my final words. Then I remembered Bella. She deserved better. She didn't deserve to be in Echo Canyon either. I couldn't go through with it, knowing that Bella would be all alone."

After a while, Anna's breathing became shallow. Then she began to snore, followed by a slow stream of snot that trickled down Hannah's neck.

As they went on, Hannah daydreamed of a fire. A simple campfire. A fire to warm her hands, and her fingers, and her toes, and her lips, and her nose. And to dry her socks, and clothes. And hot dogs and s'mores. When she closed her eyes, she could smell the smoke and see the embers travel up and out of the canyon.

For a long time, Hannah had a feeling something was following them. Maybe it was just the wind, or maybe a predator watching from the shadows, or maybe it was death, waiting in the wings, ready to take them after they took their final breath.

Hannah thought about her life. Friendships, relationships, mistakes, regrets, arguments, and dreams that never came to fruition. Everyone she loved, and everything she'd miss, and everything she'd never see again. Thoughts of her father, and Marshall, and Mark, and Casey. Nearly half her life without her sister. Half a life without that smile, that laugh, that touch telling Hannah everything was going to be okay.

Off in the distance, something lay on the canyon floor, reflecting light back to her. She stopped and stared, unsure if it was real or if she was hallucinating. At about fifteen feet away, the object came into focus. A mason jar.

When she was standing above it, she kicked it once to make sure it was real. It was. The jar was spotless, like it had just been washed. Hannah stared at it for a long time, then stepped over it and continued their death march.

"So, I've been thinking about what we're going to do

when we make it out," Hannah said, her jaw chattering. "Since you've never seen the ocean, how about we take a trip down to San Diego. What do you think about that?"

Hannah knew there wouldn't be a response, but hearing her own voice helped her sanity.

"And I've decided that I really fucked up with Mark, and I'm going to find him, and tell him that I was wrong turning down his proposal." She stopped walking. "I have to find him. I just have to ..."

When she spoke his name, all she could think about was his touch, and his lips, and his body against hers. What she wouldn't do to feel that again. She chuckled. She was so close to death, yet still thinking about being with him one last time.

Every turn gave her hope that it was their last, and the highway would suddenly appear, but each was only a false summit. In some places, the cliffs reached hundreds of feet in the air. There was no climbing out, nor going back. The only way out was straight ahead.

At some point, Hannah realized she could no longer feel her feet, like she was walking on stumps. She peered at her ankle, and the sock was now bright red. If she could've, she would've cried.

She wondered how long she could keep going. An hour? Two? Four, five, six? *No. No.* Sooner rather than later, her legs would give out. Maybe she'd try to continue, but what'd be the point? Just close her eyes and get comfortable.

At some point Hannah realized she'd forgotten about Anna on her back, and she began to concede she was losing her grasp on reality. She wondered if their trek through the canyon, and their escape, and even Anna was all in her imagination, some sort of elaborate dream.

Then she came upon two sparrows, drinking from the stream. Hannah stopped and watched. They looked back, cocked their heads at her, then spread their wings and flew up the canyon, out of sight in seconds.

At that moment, a vision of Casey's apartment came to Hannah, and in the kitchen, four decorative plates hung above the table. Two of the plates had a pig and a cow, and the other two had birds. Maybe a sparrow, or a cardinal, or a blackbird. One of the birds was holding a golf club, and the other was playing ping-pong.

Hannah had never been one to believe in the "sign from above" crap, but at that moment, seeing those birds, she was certain, delusional or not, it was Casey telling her to keep going. She wiped the mud, and sweat, and tears out of her eyes, and continued with a newfound strength.

"Anna, I'm going to keep my promise and get you out of here," Hannah whispered.

On, and on, and on they went. She marched forward for what felt like hours, when in reality it was probably closer to thirty minutes.

A light drizzle began to fall. Hannah raised her head, then opened her mouth, letting the droplets fall onto her parched tongue. As she wiped the rain out of her eyes, a glow bounced off the canyon walls through the mist. At first, she thought she was hallucinating again, but after vigorously rubbing her eyes, the light remained. She watched, trying not to blink, trying not to let it escape her sight.

With each step, the glow became bigger and brighter. Then the hum of an engine broke the silence.

With all she had left, Hannah started to jog. Minutes later, the canyon opened wide. She scrambled up a small ridge, and when she reached the top, the mining facility tower was directly in front of them.

Hannah set Anna on the ground and fell to her knees. She gazed at the tower. The blinking red light was like a beating heart.

As soon as Hannah entered the mining facility office, she dropped to her knees. The man behind the desk sprang out of his chair and stared at her like she was already dead.

"My god, what happened?" he said.

"My sister ... needs a doctor," she murmured. With nothing remaining, she fell to her side and onto the floor.

The man grabbed a jacket off the wall and placed it under her head. He began asking her questions, but the only words she could muster were "My sister," gesturing with one hand toward the door.

The man rushed out of the office and yelled something Hannah couldn't make out. She knew he must've found Anna.

Soon three, maybe four men gathered in the office. Hannah's head spun, her vision hazy. For a moment, she thought the nausea might overtake her.

Their voices became louder and clearer. Then one of the men yelled, "Fuck it, it'll be faster if I just drive them to St. George than wait for an ambulance."

When they arrived at St. George Regional, Anna was barely conscious. A sea of doctors and nurses surrounded her, and before Hannah could say anything to her, she was rushed into surgery.

Hannah was admitted, and after getting her vitals checked, she was sent to Urology with concerns of internal bleeding. After numerous tests the extent of her injuries was a kidney contusion, third-degree frostbite on all of her toes, and that her ankles were nearly raw to the bone. All collateral damage.

Once in her hospital room, she made three calls. The first to her father, whom she assured at least fifty times that she was okay, and that he didn't have to come.

"I promise I'll be home as soon as I can, and once I'm back, I'm not leaving for a long time."

The second call was to Roger.

"I knew you'd make it out of there, kid," Roger said. "Where are you at?"

"St. George Regional."

The phone went silent for a few seconds, and then Roger said, "I'll be there in about five or six hours."

"You don't have to come," Hannah said.

"I'm coming, and I don't care what you say. I just want to be there in case you have any unwanted visitors. Anyway, I still have your sister's necklace, and you've been without it far too long. I know both of us will sleep better if it's back around your neck tonight."

"Thanks, Roger."

The last phone call was to the FBI field office in Las Vegas. Before she'd finished recounting her time in Echo Canyon, agents were already being dispatched to St. George. When they arrived, they assigned round-the-clock guards at Hannah's and Anna's room, and the guards remained there for the duration of their stay.

Sometime that first night, Hannah gazed into the mirror. It had been twenty-nine days since she'd seen her own face, and it seemed distant, and she barely recognized the person looking back at her. She'd lost nearly twenty pounds—her ribcage was visible, her eyes were sunken, her cheekbones protruded, and her hair was brittle and thin.

After staring in the mirror for a long time, Hannah turned off the bathroom light, then hobbled to the window that overlooked the hospital courtyard. In the parking lot, she saw two TV news vans. The media circus regarding

Seven Day Saints, Echo Canyon, and their escape was about to commence.

She turned away and picked up a hospital cafeteria sandwich and crawled into bed. After unwrapping it, she took a bite, still daydreaming about chocolate cake and whiskey.

The story of Seven Day Saints and their escape was everywhere. Every major TV network and newspaper dispatched crews and reporters to St. George and Echo Canyon. Some members of the media were dubbing it the biggest event since the trial of O.J. Simpson.

Hannah had interview offers from Larry King, *Dateline*, Nancy Grace, and Oprah Winfrey. She turned down all of them. All she wanted was for the story to fade into obscurity, but there was no escaping it. Stories like this could live on for years, if not decades. Most likely, it would outlive her.

Rex finally got the green light to run his story on Kenneth and Echo Canyon. When he asked the governor for a quote regarding Kenneth attending his daughter's wedding, he downplayed their relationship.

"Yes, that man was on the guest list for Rachel's wedding, but so were four hundred other people. He was a top donor, but there were a lot of donors there. He was an acquaintance, but in no way would I consider us friends. I don't even recall ever saying more than a few words to him."

The Seven Day Saints compound was raided two days after Hannah and Anna's escape, in a joint effort by the FBI, ATF, US Marshals, and the Utah National Guard. Six inner circle members of Seven Day Saints, including Douglas, were arrested and held without bail. Charges ranged from kidnapping, to illegal firearms, to racketeering, to aggravated sexual assault, to sexual exploitation of a child and sex trafficking.

The compound, along with the motel and a few other structures in Echo Canyon was seized by the FBI and is scheduled to be demolished, to deter sightseers. Where once countless atrocities had taken place, there would soon be mounds of dirt and rubble.

There were also plans to auction some of the land and remaining properties, with the proceeds going to a victims' fund, which included Anna and Marie and a few hundred others. Countless civil cases were being filed against Kenneth and Seven Day Saints that would most likely bankrupt them of any remaining assets.

Three guards committed suicide, including the pair who'd stood guard when Hannah was branded. Two by gun at the compound, and the other hung himself by a bedsheet while in custody.

All cowards, Hannah thought.

Kenneth was not at the compound at the time of the raid, having fled the morning after Hannah and Anna escaped. Days after the raid, he was added to the FBI Ten Most Wanted list, and a $250,000 reward was issued for information that would lead to his capture, with a warning that he might be accompanied by loyal followers who would risk their lives to protect him.

CNN reported the FBI tip line had reports of him escaping to non-extradition countries such as Russia and China, and even one that he'd opened a commune in Somalia. Other tips had him living in an underground bunker or that he was an undercover CIA asset. In the end, it wasn't the tip line that was his demise, it was his vices.

Two months after he disappeared, he was pulled over after weaving between the lanes on I-10 outside of Jacksonville, Florida. The state trooper smelled alcohol on his breath, and saw open containers on the passenger seat. In the car, they found almost $10,000 in cash, three driver's licenses, twelve credit cards, three grams of cocaine, two bottles of OxyContin, four wigs, and numerous ATM receipts from a line of strip clubs stretching from Houston to Tallahassee.

When FBI agents questioned employees from a strip club in New Orleans, they stated Kenneth had come in four days in a row and spent the better part of the day in the club, drinking Budweiser and tipping hundreds of dollars per visit. One dancer stated that he'd asked if she'd have sex with him for $175. When she declined, he asked if she knew where he could get cocaine or crystal meth.

Kenneth denied all charges against him and told reporters, "I'm being arrested because the US government is terrified of what Seven Day Saints has evolved into. All allegations about me are fabrications created by the CIA to destroy my character."

Zach Patterson was the United States Attorney for the District of Utah, and the lead prosecutor in *United States of America Vs. Kenneth M. Pratt.*

"Are you sure you're going to be alright?" Zach said, closing the report.

Hannah nodded, looking away—she almost always avoided eye contact with him. For some strange reason, she always thought he was judging her like he was better than her. Maybe there was some truth to that. Admittedly, she was a broken person, but those mental scars had happened long before Echo Canyon.

"Okay, but if you change your mind, the offer for protection will be available."

"I just want this case to be over, and I never want to see Kenneth again."

It was Anna that worried her. Out of the frying pan and into the fire. From living in near isolation to being the key witness in the trial of the decade. But if there was one person who could make the adjustment, it was Anna. She was stronger than most.

"I'm hopeful we'll have a verdict by the end of the year. I mean, since this hit the news cycle, we've had five more women come forward, and they are all willing to testify. Including you, that makes eight. That, along with the two inner circle members of Seven Day Saints who took a plea bargain to testify against Kenneth, and the video tape we found in his personal safe, makes it a pretty airtight case."

"Are you sure about that? He has some very powerful friends."

"Yes, I am. I've been doing this for twenty years, and I've never been so confident in a case. I guarantee he is going to get convicted on most charges, and at the minimum he is looking at 250 years, so rest assured, he'll never be a free man again."

"Well, even if he spends the rest of his life in prison, that's a drop in the bucket for all the pain he's caused, and all the lives he's destroyed."

"I know," Zach said with a heavy sigh.

"What about Emily?" Hannah said, staring out the office window.

"She is a different story," he said, shaking his head. "She claims that when she arrived in Echo Canyon, she was locked in that room for five months. By the time she got out, she was afraid for her life, and her family's lives, and was too scared to disobey him." He took a second's pause. "That is directly from her lawyer."

"You mean her fucking father," Hannah said.

Hannah didn't think it was possible to hate Steve and Margaret more than she did, but she was wrong. They never once checked on her well-being or thanked her for risking her life for their daughter. The only acknowledgment of Hannah's involvement in the case was a check sent to her office. It didn't even have a thank you in the memo line. Briefly, she thought about tearing it up, but that was probably what they wanted. Instead, she vowed to never speak to them again.

He nodded. "Yes, her father, the high-profile lawyer. Well, he says she was paralyzed to Kenneth's demands. That it's a textbook case of Stockholm Syndrome."

"You know she's lying, right?"

"I know, but her story is that she was a victim, just like you—just like Anna. And her father and his legal team would draw this out for years, costing godless amounts of taxpayer money, and in the end, maybe she'd serve a year or two, and that's a big maybe." He tapped his pen on the table. "And since she hightailed it down to Mexico, I have a feeling she's not coming back to the US for a long time, and I highly doubt I'd be able to get resources to extradite her."

"Mexico? I thought she was in Denver, living with Steve and Margaret."

"Nope. About three weeks ago, she slipped out in the middle of the night. I heard she's running Seven Day Saints down in Chihuahua under Kenneth's command."

"Fucking cunt," Hannah whispered.

Zach pretended not to hear her. "Be careful, Hannah. Just because Kenneth and some of his guys are locked up doesn't mean they're not going to come after you. He has some very loyal followers who would love if you didn't testify."

"I'll be fine," Hannah said, pushing back in the chair. "Do you need anything else?"

"No, not today, but I'll be in touch." Zach escorted her to the door. "Thank you again Hannah. I've been trying to get Kenneth for a long time, and you made it happen."

"No, it was all Anna. If it wasn't for her, I'd still be locked up in that fucking dungeon."

When Hannah walked out of the federal building, Mark was sitting on a bench at the bottom of the stairs. At first, she didn't believe it was him, but then he stood up and waved. Without hesitation, she ran down the stairs, taking three at a time, then jumped into his arms, holding on for what felt like minutes.

"Oh my god, I can't believe it's you. I thought I'd never see your face again. What are you doing here?" Hannah said.

"I was in town, so I thought I'd come say hi."

"How did you freaking find me? I thought you didn't watch the news or read newspapers, because what was it? Rots your brain?"

"I don't, but you do realize this story is everywhere, and I'd have to be living at a monastery in Tibet to avoid it."

Hannah started to laugh, but it quickly turned into tears. "I've missed you so much," she whispered.

"I've missed you more than you'll ever know."

Hannah leaned back and looked into his eyes. "I promise I won't run this time."

"Good, because I'm not going to let you get away again."

Nearly seven months after their escape from Echo Canyon, and on the night before the start of the trial, Hannah visited Anna at a safe house outside of Salt Lake City. They sat in the backyard patio, sipping tea, with two federal agents ten feet away.

When Anna landed in the canyon, she'd suffered a trimalleolar fracture, or in layman's terms, a shattered ankle that required two plates, three steel pins, and countless hours of physical therapy for her to be able to walk without a limp. After two months in the hospital and inpatient rehab, she was put into federal custody until the conclusion of the trial due to death threats.

The flash flood that took Bella's life and nearly killed Hannah and Anna was a result of a storm that dropped ten inches of rain in twenty minutes northwest of Echo Canyon. In the moments before the flood reached them, Anna made the split-second decision to go for the ledge. If she hadn't, they would've been in the middle of the canyon and most likely swept away and drowned.

Two years prior to their escape, a group of seventeen had been having a family reunion at a swimming hole less than ten miles from Echo Canyon. The sun was directly overhead, and there wasn't a single cloud in the sky when a wall of water rushed toward them. All but one were swept away and drowned, and three of the bodies had never been found. Just like Hannah and Anna, they had no warning, and by the time they saw the water, it was too late.

The more Hannah thought about the family, the more she wished she could forget.

During Anna's stay in the hospital, Hannah visited every day. They watched a lot of TV. Her favorites were videos on MTV, *The Simpsons*, and *Friends*. Whenever the news came on, Anna quickly grabbed the remote and changed the channel.

Hannah taught her card games—Go Fish, Rummy, Spades, and Uno. Anna was a fast learner and soon began beating Hannah. She had her first Coke, and hot dog, and maple donut, and coffee.

Anna talked about taking her first flight, and going to her first concert, and getting her driver's license and a job, and going on dates. She also talked about Bella, and how she wanted another horse, and a Golden Retriever, and a small farm with some chickens and a goat. She was optimistic about her future, and if she was frightened, she didn't show it one bit.

"It's going to be weird seeing Kenneth again. Hopefully I don't mess up when I'm on the stand," Anna said.

"You'll be fine. Don't overthink it, and just tell the truth."

Anna nodded.

"I have a present for you," Hannah said, extending a gift bag.

"Really? I can't remember the last time I've gotten a present!"

"Well, hopefully you like it."

Anna started to open the bag, then stopped. "I'm sorry. I don't have anything for you."

Hannah smiled. "It's fine. Now open it."

Anna opened the bag carefully, then slid her hand inside and pulled out a CD: *The Bends* by Radiohead.

"Does this have 'Fake Plastic Trees' on it?"

Hannah nodded. "It does. And about ten other amazing songs."

Anna thanked her at least a dozen times, then said, "This is a CD, right? Umm, this might sound silly, but I don't know how to play it."

"I'll show you," Hannah said, laughing.

One of the agents stepped out, and both Hannah and Anna turned and waved. He nodded then lit a cigarette. Hannah stared a little longer, looking at the gun on his hip.

"Have you thought about what you wanna do once this is over and you're not surrounded by armed guards 24/7?" Hannah said, gesturing to the agent behind her.

"Yeah, I keep thinking about my time in the hospital, and all of the nurses, and it's probably like a dumb daydream, but I've been thinking about going to school to become a nurse."

"I don't think it's dumb at all. It's hard work, but it's also very rewarding. I think you'd be amazing at it."

Anna smiled.

"There was one other thing I wanted to ask."

"What?"

"Well, I was wondering if you wanted to go on a little adventure with me," Hannah said.

In a steady rhythm, Hannah spun the engagement ring around her finger. At first, the ring had felt like it was weighing down on her, making it hard to breathe, but the longer she wore it, the more she couldn't imagine waking up without it. Almost as much as Casey's necklace.

"Really? Where?"

"Didn't you say you wanted to see the ocean?"

"More than anything!"

"How about after your testimony, we go down to San Diego and I charter a boat out into the ocean and we watch the sunset?"

"Really? Are you serious?" Anna yelled.

Hannah nodded.

"I'd love that more than anything."

"So would I," Hannah said.